This is a work of fiction based loosely on Hartland Cove County, NB, Canada. Names, characters, places, and incidents are either the product of the author's imagination or are used fictitiously, and any resemblance to actual persons living or dead, business establishments, events, or locales, is entirely coincidental.

Copyright © 2019 by Kimberley Montpetit

All rights reserved.

No part of this book may be reproduced in any form or by any electronic or mechanical means, including information storage and retrieval systems, without written permission from the author, except for the use of brief quotations in a book review.

Spellbound Books

Published in the United States of America

Created with Vellum

THE NEIGHBOR'S SECRET
A SECRET BILLIONAIRE ROMANCE

KIMBERLEY MONTPETIT

FREE BOOK OFFER

When you subscribe to Kimberley's Reader Newsletter, you'll receive the romantic novel, RISKING IT ALL FOR LOVE as a Welcome Gift, plus lots of other goodies and discounts!
SUBSCRIBE AT THIS LINK:
http://eepurl.com/NBXon

DEDICATION

Dedicated to all lovers of quirky, romantic small towns!

CHAPTER 1

It was the perfect day for a wedding. After months of trying on wedding gowns, ordering invitations, and searching every bridal boutique in Toronto for the perfect shoes, Allie Strickland was ready to walk—maybe even run—down the aisle of the church and into Sean Carter's waiting arms.

She'd licked stamps to post the more than one hundred announcements until her tongue was dry. She'd suffered through at least that many long-distance phone calls with her mother that sometimes ended in arguments and tears.

But finally, that very morning, Allie grabbed a big fat red marker and made an X on the calendar.

"Mrs. Sean Carter, here I come," she whispered as she capped the pen and tossed it inside a packing box.

During their five years of dating, she and Sean had gone through grad school together, first jobs, and now Sean was climbing the ladder to become a partner with Learner & Associates law firm.

Tonight she'd be with the man of her dreams forever. No more work interruptions. No more hurried lunches. No more agonizingly long street car rides to get to one another's apartments. Lately, they would just meet somewhere in the middle for a late dinner.

Tomorrow, new renters were moving into her apartment on Bloor Street. When she and Sean returned from their honeymoon to the Bahamas, Allie would unpack the boxes sitting inside Sean's apartment and officially move in.

Allie's stomach jumped as she checked the time on her phone. Her wedding began in ninety minutes and it would take at least half of that just to get through Toronto traffic.

She sent a text to Sean and then took several deep breaths to settle her nerves while she mentally went over her wardrobe packed for fun, sun, and the beach on the way to the Episcopal Church, her brother at the wheel and her mother, sister, and best friend Marla rode in the back.

Three bikinis: red, black, and purple.

Slinky dresses for candlelit dinners.

Five pairs of shoes, including a pair of running shoes.

Lingerie and toiletries.

She couldn't *wait* to get on that plane tomorrow morning and leave work and stress and family behind.

Seven perfect days with Sean. Finally, finally, finally.

"I don't think Toronto has ever looked lovelier," Allie sighed happily, pressing her nose against the window glass like a kid.

She was excited, anxious, and terrified—and missing Sean. She hadn't seen him in three days due to his working overtime so he'd have a few days off for their honeymoon.

"I promise we'll have a longer honeymoon when I'm finished with this current trial," he'd said last week. "A cruise of the Greek Islands in autumn."

"You know all my dreams," she'd told him, throwing her arms around his neck and feeling the beat of his heart against hers.

Sean had given her a peck goodbye. "You know I have to be in the courtroom at seven a.m., Allie."

She'd frowned, turning away to stare out the window of her

apartment. It was a spectacular view of downtown and the lake. She'd been lucky to get this flat a year ago and hated to let it go, but Sean had a bigger place so she'd reluctantly given up her dream apartment.

"That case has taken over your life. *Our* lives," she said, trying not to complain. "We haven't been out in ages. We've hardly kissed in months."

"But we're getting married in a few days, Allie. Be a grown-up and get used to the hectic life of a criminal defense lawyer."

She despised those moments when he treated her like a child. But all she could say was, "But I *miss* you. Don't you miss me?"

As soon as she spoke the words, Allie chomped down on her tongue. Sentiments like those merely underscored his assessment of her as a petulant child.

"Don't sit on your dress!" Mrs. Strickland suddenly shrieked, motioning to her son that there was a red light.

"These darn no-left-turn streets," Jake muttered, braking so hard they all lunged forward. "They've got the next two streets blocked off for a 10K run."

Quickly, Allie hitched up the beaded satin wedding gown around her to prevent wrinkles on the back end.

"You simply *can't* have wrinkles when you walk down the aisle," her sister Erin said with a dose of sarcasm. "It would be, like, a crime or something."

Mrs. Strickland gave her youngest daughter a second glare and then silently held out her palm when Erin snapped her gum.

Erin stuck her wad of chewing gum in her mother's hand, smashing it down vehemently in revenge, and leaned back with a sulk.

"Thanks for the gum sacrifice," Allie told her, nudging at her sister's shoulder.

"Huh," Erin grunted, sliding another pack of spearmint contraband from her handbag.

"Look at the blue sky and enjoy the fact that there isn't ten feet of snow on the ground."

"You mean smog and obnoxiously tall concrete they call architecture."

"You only think that because you're sixteen."

"Girls!" their mother cried, craning her neck to squint at the name of the cross street. "Don't fight on your wedding day."

Jake remained stoic, his mobile giving out directions in a British accent.

"It's not *my* wedding day," Erin said, making one of her famous faces, eyes wide, nostrils flaring.

"Obviously. But today is Allie's most special day in her entire life. Be nice. Mind your manners. And *please* don't put your chewed gum on the dinner plate at the reception this evening."

"I'm not eight!" Erin crossed her arms over the deep maroon bridesmaid dress. Lower cut in the bust line than Mrs. Strickland had suggested, but nobody had listened to her protests when the wedding planning rose to extreme levels of tension.

Marla Perry, Allie's best friend since kindergarten, reached over with a tissue. "You've got a smudge of frosting on your face, Allie."

"Where?" Allie scrabbled inside her white lace-covered wedding bag for a mirror, which, of course, only held two tissues and a lipstick for refreshing. Allie had a tendency to bite off her lip color. "How could you let me leave the house like that?"

"It's just a tiny smudge," Marla assured her. "Probably cream cheese from the cinnamon roll."

"You just *had* to go and make your to-die-for cinnamon rolls on the day I wanted to be my skinniest self," Allie teased.

"I knew you'd go all day without food if I didn't give you something. And then we'd be picking you up off the floor in front of the minister when you fainted from starvation."

"Not starvation. Sugar overload. I should have had a granola bar."

"Granola bars are for birds, not real people," Marla said. "Fainting can be a means to an end. Sean can scoop you up from the cold floor and kiss you passionately."

Marla had snagged the lead role in *Romeo and Juliet* in their high school drama production class and swore she'd leave the tiny town of Heartland Cove and run away to New York City. She'd gotten as far as Toronto—which, for a Heartland Cove resident, that boasted a population of 899—was a major feat. But her fine arts degree in photography was proving difficult to find a decent paying job.

"Mom. Chill," Jake said. Miss British GPS voice told him to turn right, but when he did he hit another red light and jerked to a stop. All the women braced a hand on their seats, then adjusted dresses and jewelry.

"Warn us next time, Jake," Mrs. Strickland said, the frown deepening between her eyes.

Allie had not missed the family dynamics living in Toronto, although she sometimes got nostalgic for Heartland Cove, the town where she'd been born, worked her teen summers at the Strickland Family Fry Truck, and had her first kiss on the Bridge of Heartland Cove with a boy who told her he'd love her forever —and then promptly moved to Newfoundland three weeks later. It might as well have been Timbuktu.

After a few sexy Facebook messages, he'd posted a picture of himself with a suntanned blond girl—and disappeared from her life forever.

In Heartland Cove he'd been her only possibility for a boyfriend until she'd met Sean her senior year as an undergrad in business school.

Sean Carter was the complete opposite of the boy from tiny Heartland Cove High; tall, slim and dark-haired with smoldering eyes and a crooked grin that melted her heart.

"I think butterflies have set up permanent housekeeping in

my stomach," Allie said, glancing at the clock ticking down the minutes until she said the words, *I do.*

Mrs. Strickland patted her hand. A little bit comforting. A little bit impatiently. And a little bit sadly.

"You all right Mom?" Allie asked.

Her mother gave a wan smile, and a tug of empathy rose in Allie's chest. She'd never seen her mother wearing red lipstick. Any makeup really. Frying hamburgers and fries for the tourists that swarmed the town every day wasn't exactly conducive to glamour.

Heartland Cove's main industry were the buses that disgorged tourists three times a day to gawk at the Heartland Cove Bridge —North American's longest covered bridge.

Mrs. Strickland brushed off any discomfort she was feeling. "I'm a fish out of water in the glamour of Toronto."

"You look lovely, Mom."

Her mother was wearing a maroon sheath trimmed in lace, black pumps, pantyhose, and a ton of hairspray in a traditional middle-aged pouf. A far cry from jeans and a splattered, greasy apron.

Her cell phone began to buzz, and she recognized the familiar ring of her fiancé. "It's Sean!" she shrieked, patting at her dress and then peering along the floorboard of the car. "I can't find my phone! I talked to him just before we left the apartment. What if he got in an accident?"

"Calm down," Jake said, speeding through a light. He turned to give Allie a grin. "Knowing him, he's calling about the cop giving him a speeding ticket right about now."

"Be useful and help me find my phone, Erin!"

Her sister pressed her lips together and folded her arms across her chest, tapping one toe on the floor mat.

"Okay, sorry," Allie quickly corrected. "I'm sorry. I don't know why I'm panicking."

"Wedding day jitters," Marla said soothingly, searching under the car seats.

Allie lifted wads of satin as delicately as possible. She shook out the folds of her gown, but there was no sign of the phone. It was as if it had disappeared into another dimension.

"I wish you'd gotten married in Heartland Cove, sweetheart," Mrs. Strickland said wistfully.

The ringing had stopped by now and Allie's stomach clenched. Sean had trained her to never miss a phone call from anyone.

He always said that if they were going to excel at their careers and strive for every possible promotion, they could open their own law firm one day, Allie as office manager and head of PR. "Let no opportunity go to waste," Sean said. "Grab them all."

"My phone couldn't have vanished into thin air."

"It's probably on the floor," Erin said with a yawn.

"Can you help me reach down and get it?"

Erin heaved a second deep sigh and dug around the floor, swishing yards of satin and tulle out of her way.

"Careful of my dress!"

"I'm being careful. And . . . it's not here."

"Marla!" Allie said, panic bringing tears to her eyes.

"Don't you dare cry and mess up that makeup job. Here, grab the seat back and lift your bum." Marla ran her fingers along the leather seat under Allie's wedding gown. "Aha!" She held up the cell phone between two fingers and plopped it into Allie's lap.

"You're a lifesaver." Allie quickly checked her voicemail. Sean's deep voice spoke into her ear. "Hey, Allie, I had to run by the office to pick up a new report for this case. Mr. Thompson said I have to read it tonight. The defendant was caught—well, never mind what he was doing. I can't tell you that. But I *will* be at the church. Hitting green lights now, almost to the office."

His voice abruptly stopped and Allie stared at the lifeless phone. It would have been nice to hear an "I love you," but perhaps he'd found a parking space and run inside the office building.

"What's up?" Marla asked.

"Nothing," she lied. "Everything is fine." Inside, she couldn't help fuming. "He might be five minutes late," she added, just to prepare her family.

She hated when they complained about Sean and his awful work schedule. She didn't want to give them any more ammunition than necessary. Sean was there for all the important occasions. Right now was a critical time in his career and when they were able to be together in the same house it would be so much easier to support each other.

"At least your flight isn't until the morning," Erin said, kicking off her tight dress shoes.

"Sean will be there waiting for Allie with the minister," Marla said reassuringly.

Despite her words, the sick feeling grew in Allie's stomach.

In a low voice Marla said, "I know what you're thinking. You don't want to be embarrassed if Sean is late because you know Courtney Willis is going to be in the front row of the church, watching you marry her old boyfriend."

"The front row is reserved for family."

"That was supposed to be a rhetorical statement."

Sadly, Allie knew what she meant. "In what universe is it fair that Sean's old girlfriend gets paired up with *my* fiancé on this new high profile case?"

"In the universe of Ally Strickland," Marla said prophetically.

"That is *not* funny."

"I'm trying to get you to crack a smile. You should be glowing. You're marrying the man of your dreams—not Courtney's dreams. She lost him. Bask in the triumph. Hold your head high."

"Why did Sean invite her in the first place? We had two arguments about Courtney over the past month."

"I stamped all your wedding invitations myself. Sean sent one to every employee at the firm. He couldn't leave her out, especially when they're paired up on this case."

"Why did she RSVP? Didn't she realize it wasn't an event she was expected to actually attend?"

Before Marla could answer, Jake turned off the ignition and jumped out to open the doors all around. "We're here!"

Allie's stomach lurched. The journey to the beautiful little church was over. The moment had arrived.

In less than an hour, she would become Mrs. Sean Carter.

CHAPTER 2

Marla and Erin assisted Allie with her train along the brick walkway to the dressing rooms behind the chapel. Thirty minutes until show time and guests were already beginning to arrive.

The girls sneaked past the open doors to the sanctuary, and Allie wobbled along the uneven stones in her high heels, holding up her billowing wedding dress in both fists. She just hoped she wouldn't have blisters for the bride and groom's first dance.

Ducking under the breezeway, Allie knew it was bad luck for a bride to be seen until she appeared at the back of the church aisle on the arm of her father, but she was fairly certain that "rule" only applied to the groom.

"Put your shoes back on," Allie ordered her sister. "You're my bridesmaid."

The wedding consisted of only two attendants, her sister and best friend. Her family couldn't afford a bigger wedding party, even though Allie was helping with the expense. A fry shack in a town the size of a speck didn't bring in anywhere close to a six-figure income for her parents.

A wave of nostalgia swept over Allie. Heartland Cove was too far away for most of her childhood friends to attend. No neighbors or teachers from school. Her grandparents lived on Prince Edward Island and were too elderly to make the long trip. Besides, she'd been away at university and grad school for six years—and now two years of working. Most old friends from home only caught glimpses of each other at Christmas time when everybody was snowbound.

"Maybe we should have honeymooned on Prince Edward Island," Allie mused, touching up her makeup in the dressing room mirror.

"Oh, yeah, that would be romantic. You could visit your grandparents," Marla said wryly.

They giggled, their eyes catching in the mirror.

Marla whispered, "I hope you getting married doesn't change things."

"Marriage always changes things," Mrs. Strickland intoned with a dramatic sigh.

Marla whispered, "Pay no attention, Allie, and try to enjoy every moment of your special day—and I'll take a thousand pictures to make sure you always remember."

"I have the best wedding photographer in the country," Allie told her, watching Marla fuss with the huge camera around her neck. She was playing with the buttons and stops, shoving a hand inside her enormous handbag to check for the extra camera lenses she always carried.

Marla lifted an eyebrow in her signature gesture, whether it was amusement, mockery, or sarcasm. "Honey, you're my only gig this year so far, but you know I'm grateful."

"One day you'll be a world-renowned photographer."

"From your lips to God's ears, as they say." Marla brushed it off, ever flippant, but Allie knew she hated having to take a part-time waitressing job to make ends meet. "Okay, girl. Let's go have ourselves the best wedding of the century."

Mrs. Strickland kissed her daughter's cheek. "I hope you'll be very happy, sweetheart. Sean is a nice young man. Just don't forget to bring home some grand-babies once in awhile."

Allie laughed. "Mother! I'm barely twenty-six, there's plenty of time."

Even as she said the words, Allie realized that she and Sean hadn't talked much about having a family. Careers, deadlines, moving, and planning the wedding had taken over their lives.

Allie swallowed. "Of course, we'll have children sometime," she added when her mother's face turned crestfallen. "Actually," she added, trying to brush it off. "I don't even know if Sean likes children."

It was the wrong thing to say. Mrs. Strickland was horrified.

"Mother," Allie added hastily. "Of course he likes children. He's just—um—never been around children. He only has one older brother and no cousins."

Marla jumped in to snap a series of photos of the final moments of Allie's single status, including the glow of her eyes in the mirror of the room as she fixed her lipstick for the final time. "Erin already left to walk down the aisle and throw rose petals at the guests—"

Allie gave her a horrified look.

"I'm kidding! You're so serious today, Allie!"

Allie lifted her shoulders weakly. "Knowing my baby sister, I wouldn't put it past her to stick rose petals in people's noses. Anything to get attention."

"Okay, darlin'," Marla went on, fixing a stray hair on Allie's fancy upsweep and soft ringlets. "Now it's my turn to go walk the walk with the hunk of a best man."

She was referring to Sean's older brother, Derrick, who was a devastatingly delicious model. Lately, the man had been growing a rugged beard for a photo shoot for an outdoor adventure catalog. Marla was a sucker for a man in a rough beard and flannel.

Marla turned to Mrs. Strickland. "Go grab yourself the best front row seat, Mom."

"Yes, Marla," Allie's mother said obediently. Holding her daughter by the shoulders, she gave Allie a pensive, emotional stare, and then departed the dressing room in a bit of a daze.

But not before Marla took a few more pictures of the mother and daughter together for the forthcoming wedding album.

"Be sure you get pictures of the chapel and guests before the ceremony begins," Allie reminded her. "I want pictures of every single moment today. I'm too nervous to focus and I won't remember a thing without your photos."

"Yep, taking pictures—I'm up to one hundred—even before we left your apartment." Marla gave Allie a particular look. "You know, girl, you should think before you speak. Especially when it comes to motherhood—and grandmother-hood."

"My mother is insidious about pushing my buttons. Grandchildren! I haven't even been on my honeymoon yet!"

"See you in the chapel," Marla said, spreading out the pearl embroidered train of Allie's wedding dress so all she had to do was walk straight forward through the double doors into the main chapel. "Smile. You look stunning—and you get to see Sean in a few minutes. That should perk you up."

The room went quiet and Allie carefully turned to catch her reflection in the mirror and practice her smile. She *was* happy. Deliriously happy. Just nervous.

From outside the door, she could hear the organ softly playing. Mendelssohn's "Wedding March" was about to begin.

Allie checked her phone one last time. No messages. Sean was probably waiting for her in the chapel—phone turned off—the entire audience wondering where the bride was, the minister impatiently tapping his toe.

Her heart pounded against her ribs as she left the dressing room and made her way down the hallway. The scent of lilies and roses in her bouquet was heady and romantic.

Everything *was* perfect.

When she reached the open doors to the chapel, Allie could

see guests sitting inside the polished pews, shuffling and whispering.

A knot formed in her throat when her father spotted her and walked toward her. He was tall with distinguished gray sideburns, wearing a three-piece gray suit. He looked neither happy nor sad and Allie frowned, raising her hands in a question.

She could see heads turning to stare as Spencer Strickland moved down the aisle toward his daughter so Allie ducked out of sight back into the church corridor.

"Am I that late?" Allie said, trying to joke when her father stood in front of her. "You know promptness has never been my forte—"

Her father gave her a gentle smile and Allie craned her neck to see inside the chapel. A spectacular sunset tinted the stained glass windows, sending shards of light across the wooden floors.

Her throat closed when she spotted Erin and Marla sitting in a pew, heads bent together. They weren't walking down the aisle or standing at the dais waiting for the bride to take her place beside the groom.

"What's going on?" Allie asked. "Are we waiting for the minister, or Sean in the dressing room? What time is it?"

"You're only ten minutes late, sweetheart, but—" he stopped, his Adam's apple moving up and down as he swallowed.

"But what?" Just then, her brother Jake turned in his seat to glance back at her. The lines between his eyes deepened and his expression was not happy.

Allie's father reached out a hand to steady her when she moved to the doorway, desperate to see Sean for herself, but fully exposing herself to the guests.

All she could see was her mother's rigid back in the front pew, and the minister backing away from the dais to sit down on the seat behind the pulpit, a few scattered rose petals on the parquet floor.

Sean Carter was nowhere to be seen.

"What's happened?" she cried. "What's happened to Sean? Is he okay? Tell me he's okay, Daddy! Has there been an accident?" The questions came fast and furious and her voice echoed in the high-ceilinged chapel.

She became aware of her cell phone, heavy in the hidden pocket of her wedding gown. Allie yanked it out, willing it to ring. But instead of a missed call, there was a text message.

It said three words. **I'm sorry, babe.**

"Sean is fine," her father said, wrapping an arm around her. "The case he's on—"

"I'm so sick of hearing about that blasted case!" Allie blurted out. The chapel went silent at her sudden outburst. She spun around, lurching back into the vestibule, unable to face the staring guests.

She didn't care that her makeup was getting ruined, or that her veil had pulled away from its pins and now sat crooked on her head. She only knew that her face was pressed into her father's white shirt and she was staining it with sudden, streaming tears.

"Tell me, Daddy. What happened? You promise he's okay?"

"He's perfectly healthy, if that's what you're worried about, but the case took a turn for the worse. His client skipped out on the arraignment and nobody can find him. The district attorney said they had to hunt him down today or he'd throw the book at the guy—and the law firm."

"Sean wasn't supposed to be working today! Mr. Thompson was taking over the court appearance."

"Thompson and Sean are actually together tracking down the client." His hand was now patting her back. "Oh, honey, I'm sorry."

Allie lurched out of her father's arms. "It's our *wedding*. Somebody else should be out there tracking down their thug. This is *insane*, Daddy."

A pained look crossed her father's face. "Sean wants to make partner one day. That's the life you're going to have for a few years, honey. It's part of the game."

"I did an internship at a law firm, Daddy. I know too well, but that doesn't make it right." Allie kicked off her high heels, sending them skittering across the floor.

Dozens of eyes tried to catch sight of the bride in the foyer, every guest attempting to eavesdrop. Titters of conversation filled the chapel.

Sean was embarrassing her. *Humiliating her!*

"Sean had a choice," she said, trying not to blubber like an idiot. "Even well-respected law firms let their lawyers off on their wedding day. When will he get here?"

"Nobody knows where they are."

"He left me at the altar," Allie whispered. "How could he do this?" They had talked about this very scenario and Sean had *promised* that their wedding day—that *she*—was the most important thing to him, and work would not get in the way.

Mrs. Strickland appeared at the foyer door, followed by Jake and Marla and Erin. Their faces were a combination of shock and anger. Her brother looked ready to punch a wall.

Allie's eyes caught the minister as he was whispering to the organist. The prelude music abruptly stopped and the elderly woman blinked and gazed about the room.

Murmurs inside the chapel grew louder.

Mrs. Strickland twisted her fingers. "Spencer, we need to do something!" she hissed at her husband.

"Allie, do you want me to whisk you away?" her father gently asked.

Tears pricked at her eyes at his solicitation for her feelings. He knew she wouldn't want to face anyone, but it was already too late. The guests were rising from their pews, and then walking through the chapel doors into the garland-decorated foyer.

Stiffly, Allie sat in an upright chair, enduring the awkward embraces, the whispers of empathy, every face a blur.

Later, she wouldn't even be able to recall who had been in attendance, except for Marla standing at her side like a fierce lioness ready to take down anyone who said something snide and ugly.

One by one, the guests in their chiffon dresses and suits and ties filed out of the church. All but one young woman.

Courtney Willis. Her previous rival for Sean's affection. Of course she would come to witness Allie's moment of shame.

The woman's face was unreadable, but she had the good sense not to come over and give an air kiss, or pretend any sort of friendship.

The air crackled with unspoken words while Courtney clicked her heels down the corridor, pausing to sign the guest book with a flourish of the feather-plumed pen.

Allie had a sudden vision of driving the pen straight into the woman's jugular. "Does *she* know where Sean is? Is that where she's headed?"

Marla gripped her shoulder. "Don't start making things up to torture yourself."

Like an automaton, Allie brushed a finger across the screen of her mobile phone. A text had just appeared. Her heart thumped with both hope and dread. It was from Sean. Thirteen words.

Sorry about craziness. We'll get married another day. Not end of world. Promise.

Allie handed the phone to Marla who read it and cursed. "That son of a—"

Before her friend could finish, Allie tugged the phone out of Marla's fingers and threw it across the foyer where it smashed against the wall and broke into a dozen pieces.

CHAPTER 3

Heartland Cove County had never looked prettier. And Allie Strickland *never* thought she'd ever say that.

The town was a tiny pinprick on the map. Fewer than a thousand in population, but Heartland Cove *did* make the maps despite its minuscule size.

Every map. Too many maps.

Because Allie's hometown boasted the longest covered bridge anywhere and ever since she'd become aware of the world, Allie had lived with busloads of tourists tramping over every square inch of it.

When she was a teenager, Heartland Cove bored her out of her mind. No shopping malls, no movie theater, and a tiny K-12 school. Fishing and lobster trapping in the harbor—and the bridge—was the sum total of life.

The bridge was the topic of almost every conversation because every family was affected by the bridge and the people who came to gawk at it.

Allie knew tourists well. She'd slung fries at them for hours on end in the Strickland Family Fry Truck all through high school. Every year the tour busses got more numerous and more packed with tourists.

After living away for so many years, Allie drove down Main Street in slow motion, pausing at each intersection to peer into tiny neighborhoods of Victorian homes and shops. The bank, general store, and a bait shop. A few clapboard houses.

She marveled at how quaint it all was. Old, but with a certain early 1900s charm.

Did that happen to everybody after leaving home and becoming an adult—that your stifling home town suddenly turned old-fashioned and charming, as if fairy dust had sprinkled the countryside and turned it into Brigadoon, the town that awoke once every hundred years.

Allie pulled up in front of her childhood home. She shut off the engine, rolled down her window, and sat in the quiet. Birds twittered in the evergreen tree in her parents' front yard while she stuffed down a scream of fury that had brought her to this point in her life.

She tried to swallow, but her throat was thick. Dear Lord, she was tired of crying over Sean Carter.

Flipping down the visor to look in the mirror, Allie groaned at the sight of her puffy eyes and dark circles. She'd hardly slept the past forty-eight hours.

Marla's voice came up behind her as Allie shoved open the car door, making her jump. "Hey, you made it!"

"Home, sweet home," Allie replied, taking in the neighbor's homes with overgrown shrubbery, and pockets of patchy wildflowers.

"I wasn't sure you'd leave Toronto, but let's make the most of it." Marla grinned and lifted her camera, snapping a picture. "Hey, I could start a blog called *Diary of a Jilted Bride*. We'll chronicle your woes and broadcast it to the world."

Allie gave a snort of laughter, but admired Marla's sense of humor. "You're a piece of work."

"Hey, a girl's gotta practice if she's going to become North America's most sought after photographer."

There was a pause and then Allie said, "Today, Sean finally started calling to apologize. Begging to reschedule the wedding. As if it's all up to me. As if I'm the only one that cares in this relationship. I have no words. *No. Words!*" she added with emphasis.

Marla chewed at her lips. "Would you consider it? Still marrying him, I mean?"

"Are you suggesting I forgive him for leaving me at the altar and just go ahead and *reschedule* the wedding?" She went into full sarcasm mode. "Oh, yes, dear wedding guests, dress up again in your fancy clothes, bring a second freshly wrapped gift, drive through horrendous traffic and watch me stand at the altar all over again—while we madly hope the groom shows up this time. Forget the blog, let's just do a reality TV show!" Her face flushed red with frustration.

Marla's face filled with empathy as she opened the rear door and helped unload the suitcases and boxes Allie had brought with her.

A moment later, she looked up and put a finger on the shutter of her camera. "Let's call Hollywood and have them send up some super hot hunks. We'll make it into the funniest reality show Canada has ever seen."

"I know you're trying to get me to smile," Allie said wearily, "But the wedding cost so much, my parents and I are broke. All the vendors still need to be paid. Flowers won't last—and the catered food is in all the neighbors' freezers. It was a pain fitting everything into my car as well as my parent's vehicle, but my mother couldn't bear to throw away good food."

"You must have had to purchase a few coolers to transport the food all the way back to Heartland."

Allie nodded, pressing her lips together. "My father isn't happy about any of it, but he doesn't say much. He would never make me feel guilty."

"Make Sean pay for it. Send him the friggin' bill. It's his fault."

"Believe me, he's getting a certified letter with an itemized list. And if he thinks I'll pretend three days ago never happened and just call up the minister to find out when his next available Saturday is, he needs his head examined."

Marla clucked her tongue and wrapped an arm around Allie's shoulders while Allie leaned against the side of the car, fighting tears again.

"Do you know that Sean never even called me with any sort of explanation until four hours later? I'm not a doormat! I was supposed to be the most important person in his life."

Marla kissed Allie on the cheek, and then hugged her again. "Just assessing your true feelings."

That finally got a laugh out of her. "You don't want to know my true feelings. I think my father was ready to get his shotgun and hunt the man down."

"In Toronto?" Marla choked out. "Riiight," she added, drawing out the word with irony.

Allie hefted a small box into the crook of her arm, pulling one of the rolling suitcases behind her. "I can just see the headlines now: *Father Found Waving a Sawed-Off Shotgun at the Man Who Jilted His Daughter at the Altar*. You want to know the most infuriating part?" she added, as they hauled her stuff into the house.

Marla grimaced. "Moving back home at twenty-six and giving up your gorgeous apartment?"

"You manage to say the very thing that makes me feel so much better about myself—not." Allie set a box on the kitchen table with a thud. "Sean doesn't actually think he stood me up. He thinks he was just late." Her harsh laugh burst with ten pounds of derision. "As if the church full of guests and the entire bridal party had to exhibit a bit more patience while he was emergency hunting a client. That if we'd all only waited at the church for another six *hours*, everything would have been fine."

Marla shook her head while she pulled a suitcase into Allie's old bedroom. "The gall. The nerve."

"I think he's more ticked off that I wouldn't still agree to take our honeymoon trip with him. After all, the tickets are paid for, right? "Why can't we have a honeymoon without being married?" he said. I practically broke a second phone when he suggested that. He can't understand why I'm so angry. Why I don't want to see him."

"*Have* you seen him at all?"

"No," Allie said shortly. "If I did, I'd probably be arrested for strangling him."

Her childhood bedroom was at the front of the house and they paused as one of the daily tour buses roared past the window, filled with tourists headed to the bridge.

Allie unzipped the first suitcase. "I should probably change clothes and head over to the fry truck to help my parents. But all I want to do is flop on the bed and stare out the window with a margarita in each hand."

"Erin's there—at the fry truck, I mean," Marla said with a quick laugh. "You know, they *have* been getting along without you all these years."

Allie shook her head. "Erin's doing something else today, but I can't remember what exactly. I've never been able to keep track of my little sister."

"She's just taking advantage of your pain to run off with her friends."

Allie's cell phone buzzed and she dumped out her purse to find it.

"Hi Mom," she said, tossing clothes half-heartedly into the empty bureau. Old high school pictures were still stuffed into the edge along the mirror. The Nancy Drew collection given to her by great-aunt Clara when she was nine-years-old still sitting in the scratched-up bookcase. The familiar purple bedspread dotted with forget-me-not flowers—faded by countless launderings—covered her bed.

Allie listened to her mother for a moment, sighed, and then said goodbye. She snapped the phone off and dropped the device onto the bed, where the mattress immediately sculpted a huge dent from the impact.

"What's up?" Marla asked, taking a few pictures of Allie's time-capsule bedroom.

Allie flung clothes about, searching for an old uniform in the closet. "My darling little sister is AWOL and I have to get to the fry truck pronto. An extra bus just unloaded."

Marla gave her a pained smile. "I'll come with you."

Fifteen minutes later, Allie found herself in the middle of a déjà-vu moment, slinging fries like she'd never left home. As if she hadn't spent the past two years using her MBA as a financial manager at an actual bank.

Dad was slicing potatoes on the sanitized stainless steel table while Mom stood over the big fryers, her face serene, skin gleaming with perspiration.

When Allie arrived, Dad lifted a silent hand in greeting; Mom handed her a full-length apron, and then went back to work.

Allie grabbed the order pad and quickly ran her fingers over the numbers on the cash register—the same one they'd used since she was twelve.

"Can I help?" Marla asked.

"No, dear, we're good," Mrs. Strickland said calmly. "We have a routine."

"If you say so, but I'll get in line for a bag of fries and contribute to the cause."

Marla's summer hat flopped above her dark glasses, as if she was determined to be incognito and not recognized as a local.

Allie lifted an eyebrow. "None of the residents come around the bridge during the day. Nobody will ever know you were here."

A harried-looking father surrounded by four kids slapped

down a large bill. "Five bags of fries—and plenty of vinegar and ketchup."

While Marla disappeared to the back of the line, people of all sizes, shapes, and ages mingled about the area, buying drinks, food, or hiking down to the bridge along the tree-clustered pathways.

Allie handed over white cardboard boxes of crispy fries, blinked against the sweat threatening to drip into her eyes, and tried not to think about her canceled beach honeymoon in Sean's arms, breathtaking sunsets and cheek-to-cheek dancing every night while tropical perfume spiced the air.

Standing here in the fry shack was surreal, but the ache in her heart was a hot ball of grief that might last the rest of her life.

Allie had finally stopped responding to Sean's text messages. What was there to say? He didn't *get* it. That was the part that hurt the most.

Despite the fact that the wound was still fresh, Allie mindlessly poured hot, greasy fries into paper baskets and handed them to the next customer while coming to the realization that she wasn't as important to Sean as she wanted to be—as she should be.

The line finally began to dwindle when Allie glanced up at the final customer, a man just a few years older than herself, and without a noisy family in tow. "At last," she murmured.

His mouth curved into a smile. "Is it that bad?"

Allie's face flamed. "You heard me, eh?"

"If it helps, I do empathize. Gotta be tough slinging fries on a hot day in June in an even hotter truck with fryers and ovens going."

He pulled out his wallet, counting out bills. A black camera bag was slung over his left shoulder—broad shoulders, Allie couldn't help noticing. His build was like a professional baseball player: a trim waist in khaki-green slacks with a pullover jersey shirt showing off bulging biceps.

Allie wrenched her eyes away. She had to stop thinking about honeymoons—and everything she was missing. This guy was just another tourist taking pictures of the Heartland Cove County famous bridge. But her eyes kept roving over his physique in appraisal.

He had a nice face and a straight nose, unlike Sean who had broken his nose playing football. Photographer Guy also had eyes that looked like melting Hershey chocolate bars ready for dipping strawberries.

Allie chided herself and stared at his camera bag, an awfully nice one for a tourist. Most people used their cell phones these days to snap pictures on vacation. He was more than an amateur. Maybe she should introduce him to Marla.

"Seasoned or regular?" Allie asked, poised over the register.

"Which do you recommend?" His teeth were startling white, and his hair a deep chestnut color, wavy and cut just below his ears.

Stop it, Allie ordered herself. It was ridiculous to get burned at the altar, only to start admiring every male within a hundred yards.

"Um, I prefer seasoned," Allie answered, beginning to babble nervously. "But it's up to you—if you like a little extra saucy flavor to your fries."

The corners of his brown eyes crinkled. "Saucy fries, eh? Does that mean they're impertinent or merely cheeky?"

"I mean spicy—kind of like barbecue—but not hot. Just—" Allie broke off. She was stumbling over her words like a teenager who'd never had a boyfriend.

"Sorry," he said, pushing a twenty toward her, that crooked smile crossing his lips again. "I couldn't resist."

Allie deliberately looked away lest she was taken in by that disarming smile, punching buttons on the cash register. She pushed his change from the twenty across the counter.

He reached out and slid it back again. "Keep the change."

"What are you talking about? A twenty could have bought you four trays of fries."

He gazed at her, and she finally got it. He was giving her a tip. Feeling stupid, Allie felt heat rise up her face again. "Oh, right. It's, um, been awhile . . ." Her voice petered out, as if she'd just forgotten how to speak.

"First group of the day done," Mom announced, loosening her apron and pushing back her damp hair. "I've got cold lemonade when you're ready, Allie."

"Allie," the stranger repeated and Allie cursed her mother.

Was this guy flirting, or just being annoying?

"You'd better gobble down those fries and get your photos taken before the busses leave," Allie told him.

"How do you know I'm headed to the bridge?"

"That top-of-the-line camera is a dead giveaway that you came here to take pictures."

He glanced down at his expensive camera. Was he really a photographer, or an amateur with too much money? "Right. I'll go shoot some pictures now. As soon as I finish these delicious seasoned fries."

"Saucy," Allie said, not letting him get away with flirting.

"Touché." He quirked an eyebrow and then added, "See you around Allie."

"Cheeky dude." Allie tried not to scrutinize him while he walked across the grass toward the bridge. Tried not to stare at his physique, mentally comparing him to Sean—while guilt washed over her as if she were cheating on her husband. Which totally didn't make sense.

Sean Carter was not her husband. He wasn't even her fiancé any longer. Allie's shoulders slumped over the cash register.

What an outrageously depressing week this had been already, and it was only Tuesday.

CHAPTER 4

The first night home was painful and awkward. Allie's canceled wedding with all of its expense and embarrassment was like the proverbial elephant—or dead body—in the living room.

Mr. and Mrs. Strickland had brought home the lilies and roses—now wilting on every table and chair throughout the main floor of the small house, including rows of them along the porch railings.

Uneaten wedding food was stuffed into the overflowing refrigerator and deep freeze.

"After a long day at the fry shack," Allie said, picking at her plate with a fork. "We are now eating three-day old wedding hors'doeuvres, meat and cheese plates, and crackers and dip."

The wedding cake with its whipped butter cream frosting and blood red roses, a layer of Sean's favorite dark chocolate hidden inside the middle tier—was sitting in all its sad glory on the washing machine—a spot where Allie wouldn't have to look at it ten times a day.

"At least I didn't have to cook," her mother said, bringing out a veggie tray and peeling back the plastic wrap. "Anybody want ranch dressing to go with the carrots and celery sticks?"

Allie pushed her plate away, at the same time she wanted to secretly gorge on the wedding cake. She needed a sugar rush.

"I can't eat anymore," she finally said.

Her mother touched her hand. "You'll feel better tomorrow. The sun will come up again."

"Mother, your Pollyanna sentiments are not helping my mood."

"Mooning about the house and being negative only begets more negativity."

Allie crashed her chair back against the wall. "If I see one more plate of old wedding food, I'll throw myself off the leaky roof. I know you're only trying to be understanding, Mom, but it's just—just—" she broke off, pressing her thumbs into her burning eyes."

"Now Allie," Dad said, the bastion of strength and goodwill in her life.

"Not you, too, Dad." Allie gulped down a glass of water and stared out the window to the backyard with its overgrown shrubbery and tall silver birch. "Let me be angry, okay? Don't try to placate me or speak to me like I'm going to fall apart—even if I am about to fall apart."

Her mother's face was forlorn, as if Allie had rejected *her*.

"Maybe I shouldn't have come home," she said quietly, her chest tightening.

"Come back to the table," Dad cajoled. "Let's talk about it. Help you make plans after this—this little vacation away from your job and Toronto life."

"See? That's the problem. I *used* to have a life in Toronto and my Heartland Cove life is too far in the past so now I have neither. Nothing is the same. I'm not a kid and I'm not an adult either, if I'm living here. Maybe I shouldn't have taken a leave of absence from work. In Toronto I could have buried myself in work, but I was afraid of running into Sean."

She could see her father silently agreeing.

"What are you saying?" Mom asked with a quiver in her voice.

"I can't return to the city like nothing ever happened. I loved my apartment, but I'd already given it up to create a new home with Sean. Now that's gone. Coming home feels like I've regressed back to a kid. I have to be on my own."

"What are you proposing, Allie?" Dad asked, but Allie could tell he already knew what she was implying. Of both her parents, Dad had always seemed to miss her the most when she left for university. He was the steady rock, but right now he couldn't help her. Only she could figure this out.

"I'm not proposing anything at the moment, but I *am* going for a walk."

Her mother finished clearing the table and gave her a quick smile as though Allie were still thirteen years old and had merely had a fight with Erin. "The fresh air will do you good."

Allie threw the front door closed and stomped down the porch. Could her mother be any more patronizing? As if a round of fresh air and walking the block would make everything all better.

It was only seven o'clock so Allie had a good two hours before the sun set. She found herself walking fast, and then running along the asphalt into the older part of Heartland. There were no concrete sidewalks like Toronto had, only gravel along the pavement, and older homes set back off the road.

After an hour, Allie's thighs began to ache from the activity, despite the fact that she wore heels every day to work and walked several blocks to Toronto's commuter train.

The sun sank lower, reflecting gold across the river. Thick trees curved around her, as if they were sheltering her. Self-doubts tortured her mind which was why she was tired and ornery. Not sleeping well did nothing for your mood, temperament, or looks.

Did Sean have some other woman? Someone he didn't have the guts to admit to Allie about?

Self-doubt was one thing, but suspecting he was having an affair made Allie want to fall to the earth in a huge, messy heap.

She was getting tired and she'd also forgotten her phone back at the house. If she could call, Dad would rescue her in a heartbeat—and bought her ice cream on the way home.

Oh, to be young again without all these life-altering issues.

When Allie raised her head again, she noticed lights flickering through the trees just off the road to her right. Someone had just turned on a porch light.

That's when she saw the "For Rent" sign on the house next door.

Excitement surged through her at the sudden idea. Renting her own little place would give her a chance to escape her claustrophobic family. She could be independent again—and hopefully heal the emptiness in her heart.

Allie trudged up the pathway to the old Victorian. Shades were drawn across the first floor windows—and the second story—but the porch light glowed bright like a beacon.

The house had probably been built more than a hundred years ago. If it had plumbing problems they wouldn't be her concern if she were only renting. Allie had a little savings, enough for the leave of absence her boss had insisted on, and the thought of having her own place was enough to make her feel exhilarated: a house she could decorate, a little house of her own to distract her, at least for a month or two.

Allie crossed her fingers while she walked up the stone path, overgrown with weeds, to the porch. "Please don't insist on a year lease," she said aloud.

The knot in her chest loosened when she saw the porch swing. Allie slid her palm across the chain link that anchored the swing to the eaves. She could already imagine herself sitting here in the evening reading a novel.

A scattering of leaves rattled across the wooden porch slats while a light breeze ruffled the surrounding trees that enclosed the property.

The house definitely needed a paint job, and the yard needed weeding and raking. Maybe she could work out a deal with the owner.

There was a decorative knocker on the front door and Allie lifted it and let the tarnished brass ring rap against the plate four times.

While she waited, she turned back toward the road, observing that the nearest neighbors were about three acres to the west. Their lights blazed in the windows beyond the fence lines.

When nobody answered, Allie knocked again, louder this time. The wind picked up, scattering a pile of dry brown leaves left un-raked from the previous autumn.

It finally dawned on her that the house might not currently be inhabited.

Cupping her hands against the front windows, she tried to peer past the curtains. No light seeped through.

After trying the knocker one last time, Allie moved off the porch and looked into the side windows. Not a smidgen of light.

Back in the front yard, Allie memorized the handwritten phone number on the For Rent sign.

The streets were darkening by the time Allie reached home, streetlights popping on one by one.

"Allie, that you?" her father called from the den.

"Yes, it's me."

"Darling, come here," her mother called next and Allie heard the television paused and muted when she entered the room.

"I'm going to bed, I'm beat. And I need a shower after all that fry slinging."

Her mother gazed at her as if trying to read her mind. "Are you alright, Allie? You were gone a long time."

"I'm perfectly fine. Just exhausted."

"If you say so." Mrs. Strickland was never convinced.

"Goodnight, sweetie," her dad said, allowing her to slip out when he raised the volume again. "See you bright and early."

Once she was in her room, Allie dialed the phone number from the yard sign. It rang three times before a a woman's voice came on. "You've reached the offices of Heartland Realtors. Please leave your name, phone number, and a brief message and we'll return your call as soon as possible."

Allie was jubilant. The house was unoccupied and represented by a rental company. Quickly, she left a message and then jumped in the shower, feeling optimistic for the first time since Saturday's betrayal.

CHAPTER 5

By the next evening, Allie was hauling her suitcases and boxes up the driveway of the rental house. The Victorian had been empty for the past year and was happily rented by the time Allie departed Heartland Realtors during her lunch hour.

Viola Stark explained that the owner hoped to return sometime in the next year and refurbish the place, to either sell it or to live in it again.

"Perfect," Allie told her. "I only want it for the summer."

After she signed the contract and handed over a check for the deposit and first month's rent, Viola informed Allie that she could move in anytime.

"And yes, it's furnished," she said to Allie's next question. "No guarantees on the state of the interior so bring your mop and bucket."

"Am I allowed to plant flowers or clean up the yard?"

"Good grief, yes! We're short-staffed this summer and I certainly don't have time or inclination to keep up with every one of my properties. It's all I can do to keep the roof from falling in and the plumbing working."

On that encouraging note, Allie had returned to the fry shack, a jump of excitement in her stomach and a bigger smile on her face than she'd had in days.

Marla helped her move, and boxed up the few pictures and books and alarm clock she'd brought from Toronto. All of her possessions and furniture had been ready to go into Sean's apartment, but were quickly routed to a storage unit after the fiasco of her wedding day.

Her mother was not happy about her decision to move out. "I'd hoped to have you all to myself this summer," she said forlornly when the final tour bus, belching black smoke, roared out of town. "At least for a little while," she added while Allie packed the last of her clothes back into her suitcases.

And then when Allie was loading her car, "But you barely got home. Don't I get you for more than three days after all the drama and tragedy?"

Allie zipped up her second suitcase with a snap. "Mother, there wasn't a tragedy. Nobody died."

"Well, you know what I mean."

"I do, but it's been too long that I've been on my own. I'm going to scream if I stay here."

Her mother's face fell, a hurt expression in her eyes. "I didn't realize you felt that way about us."

"I'll see you every single day at the family business, remember?"

Mrs. Strickland slowly nodded. "Well, I guess there's that."

Allie's father said, "I'll come over on Saturday and help you mow the weeds."

"Thanks, Dad," she told him, kissing his cheek. "And, Mom," Allie added when she was walking out the door to the car, "Remember, I wasn't supposed to be home this summer at all. I was supposed to be married. On my honeymoon. Unpacking wedding silver and matching monogrammed towels in my new home."

The door closed behind her and Marla said, "Ouch. That was blunt."

"Did I come on too strong?" Allie felt a twinge of guilt.

Marla popped the trunk. "Sometimes parents need to hear it straight and uncensored. And, actually, everything you said was true."

"I'll be awake all night wondering if my mother is crying into her pillow," Allie said as they drove the two miles to the Victorian house.

"Stop with the guilt," Marla ordered. "You're five minutes from home." She opened the passenger door and shaded her eyes against the setting sun. "This is one amazing house, Allie. I'm jealous."

"You can visit anytime. We'll do a sleepover."

Marla laughed. "I'll bring the popcorn and movies."

The rest of the evening was spent hanging clothes, filling drawers, and putting fresh sheets on the master bedroom mattress that was in surprisingly good shape.

The furniture pieces placed in each room were Victorian replicas. Allie loved it, and allowed a feeling of euphoria to overshadow all the hurt that had weighed her down like a stone over the past week.

"Want to get some dinner?" Marla asked after she'd explored nook and cranny of the old house.

There were three bedrooms upstairs, two full modern bathrooms, a parlor, sitting room and a guest suite downstairs with a modern kitchen.

French doors opened onto a patio where a tangled backyard lay full of overgrown shrubs and neglected rose bushes.

Allie stifled a yawn. "After being on my feet all day I'm dying for a shower, and then bed. Rain check for Friday night? And is there somewhere exciting within a two hour drive? I'm in serious need of drowning my sorrows for a night."

"I hear they have live music during the summer months over in Fredericton."

"That's a new one. Guess I've been away from home longer than I thought."

"Yeah," Marla said, going quiet. Her face was thoughtful. "You have."

Allie reached out to embrace her. "I've missed you."

"Fiancés and weddings will do that to a girl."

Allie tried not to think about that. She had her own place, her own space, her own life back—even if those were just the first of many baby steps to heal her heart. "Okay, my BFF, I'm going to wander my new house, touch all the furniture, make a cup of tea, and then take a long soaking bath."

"Ditto for me—except the house part." With a grin, Marla waggled her fingers in goodbye and opened the front door.

Allie stood on the porch to see her off, and then fished the car keys out of her pocket to hit the lock button to her own vehicle. It gave a brief beep and then she climbed the three stairs back inside—but not before pulling down the For Rent sign sitting in the window.

Perhaps she'd bribe Erin to weed for a few hours. That would help the house look occupied.

Allie pressed her back against the front door with a happy sigh. Her very own *house.* Not an apartment—a house with a porch and a backyard—a backyard that even had a fountain, if she could get the clogged pipes cleaned out.

Viola Stark had sent over a cleaning woman while Allie had been at work and the cherry wood tables and upholstery arms glowed, the air smelling faintly of lemon polish. Not a speck of dust anywhere, including freshly vacuumed rugs and a bathroom that was pristine, despite faded curtains covered with yellow daffodils from the 80s.

Allie prepared a steaming cup of orange blossom tea and took it upstairs, securing the doors and turning out the lights on her way up.

Kicking off her shoes, she ran the bath, squirting a stream of bubble soap under the pounding faucet. Cool air wafted through one of the side windows of the master suite, making her skin prickle, but the freshness revived her after such a long day.

She closed the bathroom door, stripped off her sweat-stained greasy clothes, and stepped into the water, her muscles finally relaxing as she leaned back against the porcelain.

Once she finished drinking the tea, Allie's eyes closed. Her thoughts grew heavy. Images of the past several days insisted on rolling across her mind; the wedding guests' shocked faces, whispering behind their hands.

Then came the phone calls to her boss who was kind enough to insist she take a short leave of absence, then hiring a moving van to put her things into storage.

Even if it was only temporary, this house was a blessing. A refuge. A place to heal, alone.

Allie was almost asleep, the water cooling, her arm dangling off the edge of the tub. She told herself she needed to go to bed, but was too lazy to actually reach for her robe lying in a heap on the fuzzy rug.

Her mind drifted, spinning with a hundred thoughts about how to get her revenge on Sean when the door to the bathroom suddenly swung open, banging against the wall.

A man burst inside and Allie's eyes widened in shock. His presence filled the tiny room, his body tall and muscular and looming. A shriek rose from her throat. "Who the hell are you? Get out! Stay away from me!"

Her arm flung outward as she reached for her robe because the towel was too far away, but when she half-way rose to retrieve the robe she let out a shriek, glancing down to see soap bubbles clinging to her breasts and thighs.

Legs shaking, Allie tried not to slip on the bottom of the slick porcelain tub while she snatched at the shower curtain to wrap around herself, but the floppy curtain smacked against the teacup which flew off the edge of the tub and smashed against the wall in a dozen pieces.

"Get out!" she screamed. "Get out of my house or I'll call the police! You pervert! If you come any closer, I swear I will kill you!"

The man reared back, as if shocked by her words. Then he said, "Who the hell are *you?*"

"How dare you barge into *my* house—into *my* bathroom—" her voice broke off while she gulped air, wondering how she was going to get past him to call the police. "Are you some kind of freaking felon here to attack me?"

As if in a daze, the man gazed about the bathing area, taking in the smashed teacup as well as the piles of makeup and hair products strewn across the countertop like he'd accidentally stumbled into a beauty shop.

He threw up his hands as if to ward off a flying curling iron. *"Attack you?* Are you nuts?"

Recognition suddenly dawned as she realized who he was. She sputtered, *"You!"*

The man sucked in a sudden breath, his deep brown eyes staring at her face. "It's—*you!*" he flung back at her.

"You're that—that—" Allie couldn't even finish a coherent sentence.

This man—this intruder—was the guy from the fry shack. The last customer from yesterday. The guy who'd flirted with her over a bag of stupid seasoned fries.

CHAPTER 6

"What are you doing in my house?" she yelped again. "And what are you still doing in Heartland Cove? Didn't you take the tourist bus out of town?! Are you stalking me?" She moaned at the last one, biting her lip and tasting blood at the thought of it.

Allie's mind ran through the myriad of possibilities. Why had she left her cell phone in the bedroom? "Oh, dear God, help me," she whimpered, moving as far away from him as she could, the plastic shower curtain wrapped around her torso as her last means of protection.

She had no weapon, and if she moved toward the counter to grab something he'd have her down on the floor before she could take another breath.

"I never left town," he said. Confusion ran across his features as he took in the array of her belongings all over the master suite, his head swiveling back and forth between the makeup products on the counter and her open suitcases and boxes in the bedroom.

He obviously hadn't expected her to be here. He was obviously completely psycho nuts. He must have purposely hid from the tourist bus and stayed in Heartland Cove for a nefarious reason.

"You just proved my point." Allie willed herself not to faint. *"Now get out of my bathroom!"*

"Right. Sorry," he stuttered. "Actually, I didn't mean to—I didn't expect—"

"GET OUT!"

Her screech finally moved him to action. After stumbling back through the door, he slammed it closed.

"LOCK IT!"

A male hand came around the edge of the door and punched the button on the door handle, and then shut it again, rattling the knob to prove that it was locked.

The bathroom went dead quiet. Only the rippling sound of the bath water broke the silence.

Slowly, Allie pushed aside the clammy curtain and scooped up a towel from the floor. She flung it around her naked body, staring death at the door, terrified it would suddenly open again.

Once more, Allie pictured her cell phone lying on the night table beside the queen-sized bed.

Shaking, she scrambled back into her dirty work clothes from the day. Unfortunately, the clothes wardrobe was in the bedroom and not the bathroom, but stinky clothes were the least of her worries. How had this man gotten into the house? He had to have broken in. Had he been stalking her since yesterday?

"I have to call the police," Allie moaned. He hadn't attacked her yet, even when he'd had the opportunity, but right now that was small comfort.

Rifling through the bathroom drawers, the linen armoire, and then the cupboard under the vanity, Allie finally came up with a wrench. Probably forgotten after someone had fixed the leaky faucet.

Armed, Allie felt much better. Except was *he* armed, too?

Allie yelled through the door, "When I open this door I expect you to be gone. Gone, you understand? I never want to see you again. Ever! And I'm calling the police. And I'm filing charges for breaking and entering."

She wiped at her nose with the back of her hand, trying not to cry. Slowly, she cracked open the door, the wrench raised in one hand. Ready to slam the door closed again if he lunged at her.

The lamp besides her bed was still lit. The window was still open, too. Night air drifted along the floorboards.

Actually, there wasn't a hint of noise or footsteps coming from the bedroom at all. Allie waited another few moments, holding her breath. She wished she knew where the noisy floorboards were so she could move forward undetected.

After several long moments, it appeared he really had gone. Maybe he was a wacko and had just been released from a mental hospital.

Although yesterday he'd seemed perfectly normal, calmly eating his food while he sauntered toward the bridge with his expensive camera hanging from his shoulder.

Didn't psychiatrists say that sociopaths often appeared perfectly normal and charming? Right before they scammed you or raped you? There were entire books written about sociopaths and how to spot them. Allie wished she'd bothered to read one. Or maybe it was psychopaths that became murderers. She couldn't remember.

Allie gripped the wrench tighter before pushing the bathroom door wider and peering around the corner.

The air whooshed out of her lungs. The guy—man—intruder—psychopath—was sitting in the rocking chair near the picture window overlooking the rear gardens.

"What the—?" Allie started. "You were supposed to be gone!"

He jumped up, holding up his hands as if to ward her off. "I promise I'm not an intruder or a robber," he began.

How had he known what Allie had just been thinking? She raised the wrench above her head while scrambling to her phone.

"I'm calling the police right now, and if you aren't out of this house in the next three seconds, I'm hitting you over the head with my weapon."

He surveyed the rusted old wrench while he rose from the rocking chair. "My grandmother used to hold me on her lap in this very chair when I was a little boy. She'd tell me stories about—"

"Are you certifiably insane now? This isn't your house."

He spread his hands, a hang-dog look of innocence on his features, but he wasn't fooling her.

"Stay where you are!" Allie fumbled with the phone to dial emergency services. "You're trying to trick me or confuse me."

He shook his head, thick dark hair falling over his eyes. "Please. I'm just as shocked to see you here as you are to see me."

"I don't have a *clue* who you are. And shocked is an understatement. You just tried to attack me in the bathtub!"

"Now, you know that's not true," he said, making his voice calm and reasonable.

"No, you don't get to do that," Allie ordered, waving her weapon again. "You don't get to act calm and reasonable after barging in on me in the bathtub."

A dimple in his left cheek appeared when he gave a faint smile. "Are you squatting in my house? Pretending to secretly live here?"

"What in the world are you talking about?"

"I see very few of your personal belongings and I know the furniture isn't yours, nor are the dishes in the cupboard."

"The house came furnished and I just arrived this evening."

"Ah, a brand *new* house squatter."

"I am not living here rent free. I have no idea why you would think that."

He scanned her grease and food-stained clothes. "Ah, yes. The Strickland Family Fry Shack," he noted, pointing at the business tag on her work shirt.

"Didn't you notice my car in the driveway?"

"I thought someone was just taking advantage of an empty house—and empty driveway."

"You need to leave, or haven't I made myself clear enough? I'm renting this house. Legally. I paid first and last month's rent and a deposit."

He raised his eyebrows and cocked his chin, looking suddenly very adorable. Allie shook her head to clear her brain.

"You paid rent?" he echoed. "Now that's very interesting. May I borrow your phone?"

He began to walk forward and Allie raised her weapon once more. "Stay where you are. I know that trick."

"I assure you I am not playing tricks on you. I'm not here to hurt you. I'm just as surprised as you are. But it's all beginning to make sense now. Did you sign a lease with Heartland Realty?"

"I most certainly did. The house is mine."

He shook his head, smiling broadly now. "No, actually, the house is mine."

"Dear Lord in heaven, you are annoying. And you may not use my phone."

"Okay, fine, I understand. I was just trying to avoid walking back down to my car. My car that's parked right behind yours in the driveway."

Cautiously, Allie peered out through the lace curtains, feeling like she was in a spy movie. Sure enough, there was a brand new BMW parked right behind her five-year-old Pontiac with the slight dent from a hit and run in the parking garage in Toronto.

She fought down a surge of panic. Her escape vehicle was blocked. Wiping perspiration from her eyes, Allie punched the buttons on her phone again to bring up the screen.

The man came two steps closer, making Allie dizzy. "I'm going downstairs now," he said. "Will you also please call the emergency number at Heartland Realty? Talk to Viola Stark and tell her I'm here." He strode out the door, heading downstairs.

"Wait a minute!" Allie screeched. "How do you know Viola Stark is at the realtor office? Who *are* you?"

"I'm sorry I didn't introduce myself. I actually meant to, but our conversation turned a little confusing."

"I don't have *conversations* with strange men who barge into my bathroom unannounced and uninvited," Allie said icily, shaking the wrench in a threatening manner so he would know that she was royally pissed and terrorized.

"You're right. Of course you're right, Miss Strickland, and I profusely apologize. It will never happen again. But we do have a problem here."

He proceeded downstairs while Allie muttered, "A problem? You got that right, buddy."

She slammed the bedroom door shut and locked it. Then she snatched up her lease papers and called the after-hours number for the realtor. After speaking with an emergency operator, she left her number for Viola Stark, who returned the call within ten minutes.

Allie answered the ring with a sigh of relief. If this guy wasn't legit in some way; a maintenance guy, an old friend of Viola's, a confused neighbor (although it would be unlikely that he had dementia at the ripe old age of approximately thirty), she planned to finish that 911 call to the local constable, Sergeant Bowman.

"Hello, Allie, what can I do for you?" came Viola's voice. "How's the move-in going?"

"A man just walked in on me taking a bath."

"Oh, my goodness! That's terrible. Did you call the police? Did he hurt you?"

"Not yet. I grabbed a wrench under the sink and then I recognized him from the tour bus yesterday."

"Now that's peculiar . . ." Viola began.

"Then he started talking about the rocking chair and his grandmother and he left—after he told me to call you. He knew your name. That wouldn't be difficult since he could have easily scoped out the house earlier and planned this entire thing."

"Wait, Allie, I'm getting another call—" Viola put her on hold.

Allie stared at the phone. "You're putting me on hold after what I just told you?"

There was silence.

"She *did* put me on hold," Allie spit out. "I feel like I've walked into a Twilight Zone episode."

A moment later, Viola was back, slightly out of breath. "Allie, can you describe this guy?"

"Well, he's about six foot two or three, shaggy dark brown hair, brown eyes."

"Does he have a dimple in his left cheek?"

"I—I—what sort of a question is that! I was too terrified to admire any dimples he may or may not possess on his face."

Which was a lie, of course, but Viola Stark didn't need to know that.

Viola gave a knowing laugh. "Did he mention that his grandmother used to live there?"

Allie sniffed. "He may have."

"Oh, honey, that's Benjamin Ethan Miles III. I just got off the phone with him while I put you on hold. He says he's standing in the front yard right now. He's driving a BMW with a sun roof. Blue. Yeah, he goes by Ethan Smith."

"What did you say?" Allie asked, thoroughly confused now. "Benjamin Ethan Miles the *third?*" That explained everything. The intruder was a pretentious jerk, assuming he was so privileged to just walk into a house without checking to see if the place was occupied.

Surreptitiously, she walked back to the window and pushed aside the curtains. The man was still there, and yes, he was pacing the stone path between his BMW and the porch, his ear pressed to a phone. The one he'd gone to retrieve from his car.

"Ethan Smith, eh?" Allie said with sarcasm.

Viola took a breath. "I'm so sorry, Allie, I completely forgot he was coming into town this week. He's—well, never mind why, it doesn't matter, but yes, the house does belong to him. It slipped my mind that it wasn't available until next week. I just got so excited to rent it after all this time. Silly me."

"Silly you," Allie repeated in a low voice. Louder, she said, "Well, this Miles the third dude probably took ten years off my life."

Viola apologized some more. "We'll take off the rent charges for your first month. How does that sound?" When Allie didn't respond, Viola added, papers rustling in the background, "That particular house is actually rent-free for the rest of the summer! How about that?"

Allie smiled to herself. Rent free would certainly help her bank account considering she wasn't pulling a paycheck for quite a a few weeks. The leave of absence was without pay, but her boss had assured Allie she had a job when she returned to Toronto.

"Allie, I know Ben—I mean, Ethan. He would insist on these terms. He's actually very kind. A very good man. So generous."

"Honestly, I couldn't care less what kind of a man he is," Allie interrupted. "He should have seen the lights on and known someone was here."

Viola gave an indulgent sigh. "I'm sure he's distracted. You see, his grandmother is ill, and, well, the house was hers. The Miles family built it over a hundred years ago. Lots of family history there—Heartland Cove history."

"Honestly, I couldn't care less," Allie repeated. "I just need some sleep. And I want him to go away. I suppose he has keys. That's how he got inside the house without me being aware of it."

"Exactly," Viola said in her annoyingly calm voice. "I'll call him back and talk to him. Don't you worry, the entire Miles family is wonderful and they have been extremely generous with the county. I assure you."

As if Allie cared about their generosity or legacy at the

moment. It had never affected the Strickland family, and probably never would.

Downstairs, the doorbell rang.

Viola must have heard the sound of the Westminster chime through the receiver because she asked, "Is that Ethan?"

"If it is, I don't know why he bothers ringing the bell," Allie said, her sarcasm a mile thick. "After all, he barged in earlier without a knock or a hello."

She glanced down into the front yard again. A set of headlights was parked along the edge of the road, the engine obviously running. A shadow of a figure sat in the driver's seat

"Now who's arrived?" Allie fumed. "This house is turning into Grand Central Station."

"Call me if you need anything else," Viola said gaily. "Enjoy the house!"

"You can be sure I will do exactly that. I might even be calling again in five minutes from now," Allie said, and clicked off the call with a good hard punch of her thumb.

CHAPTER 7

Allie cautiously descended the mahogany staircase to the front hall, prepping her phone to make a quick 911 call.

Ethan—or Benjamin—was nowhere to be seen. Her stomach fluttered in anticipation, or fear, she couldn't really define it. Was he still outside, or had he returned inside?

She didn't know whether to be discomfited by the fact that he owned the house and had opened the bathroom door on her thinking *she* was an intruder, or angry that he hadn't called out his presence—or was too obtuse to realize a woman was in the house. Hadn't her open suitcase lying on the bed and half full of feminine apparel screamed that fact?

Still, she wanted to know where he was. And it wasn't just because she wanted to hit him over the head with a rusted wrench. The realization was disconcerting, a contradiction in what she should be doing, which was locking the bedroom door and calling the police to arrest him.

But had this Ethan guy broken the law? Not exactly. Only a terrifying misunderstanding that had aged her at least five years.

By the time she opened the front door after the Westminster

chime doorbell had repeated twice again, Allie's jaw dropped. "Mother! What are you doing here?"

Mrs. Strickland had the good sense to look abashed. "I just made this blueberry crumble cake with that cinnamon butter topping you love so much and I thought, what a perfect housewarming gesture."

She beamed at her eldest daughter while Allie inwardly groaned. "I've been here for all of about four hours, Mom. I've been trying to get to bed for the past hour."

Mrs. Strickland shook her graying blonde hair out of her eyes and stepped inside. "I know it's late, but when I get the urge to bake I just can't help myself."

Allie knew better than to believe her mother's fibs. She wanted to see the house and couldn't wait for Allie to get settled and receive a personal invitation.

"Who's in the car? Dad?"

Her mother's shoulders lifted in a helpless gesture. "He wasn't too happy about this actually. He's even wearing his slippers, which is always difficult when driving a stick shift."

Allie tried not to snort with laughter. She could only shake her head at her silly parents.

"We had to come right away because blueberry crumble is best eaten warm. Too bad you don't have any ice cream to make it a la mode."

Allie couldn't help laughing. "I don't normally go grocery shopping at ten o'clock at night."

"Of course, you don't." Gripping the ceramic dish with her hot pads, Mrs. Strickland took the time to scan Allie up and down, her eyes zeroing in on the grease stains still adorning her work clothes. "I think you forgot to shower before getting ready for bed, dear. Do you have a clean uniform for tomorrow?"

"Yes, I have a clean uniform. Now don't keep Dad waiting. If he honks the horn the neighbors will be upset."

Her mother laughed, reminding Allie of Viola Stark on the

phone just moments before. "People in Heartland Cove don't bang down people's doors."

After her mother stepped inside, Allie gave a quick intake of air and then turned to block her mother's view of the dining area beyond the front room—because Benjamin Ethan Miles had suddenly appeared in the kitchen. He'd probably come in through the back door. With a key.

Quickly, he put a finger to his mouth, clearly asking Allie not to give him away. She gave him a glare and then turned back to her mother.

"Let me take this dessert off your hands." Without waiting for an answer, Allie took the cake into the kitchen so her mother would remain in the front room, striding forward so fast Ethan had to scurry backward into the dark sitting room opposite so as not to be seen.

She stared him down with a dose of wrath and fury, but not before she'd seen the dimple deepening his left cheek in a blatant show of amusement.

So Viola Stark was correct. This man was actually Benjamin Ethan Miles *the third*.

Allie set the cake on the counter and returned to the front hall to tell her mother goodbye, but not before shooting another deadly glare into the adjoining sitting room. Ethan held up his hands in mock innocence, a boyish grin on his lips.

Allie wanted to scream at his flippancy. Why hadn't the man left already!

"Goodnight, Mom," she said, taking her mother's arm and pulling her out to the front porch. She gave a wave to her father, and he returned the wave through the tinted car windows.

Allie didn't move from the porch until her mother had slid into the passenger side.

If her mother—or father—caught sight of this guy they'd have a fit and there was no way Allie could explain his presence. Especially this late at night. Especially when she'd just moved in. And especially when she was still crying over an ex-fiancé.

After her parent's car drove away, Allie walked back inside, musing on the sudden realization that she hadn't shed a single tear all day. For the first time in five days. Two days ago she was sure she'd never stop weeping for the rest of her life.

An evening breeze rattled the leaves of the tree shading the porch swing and she reached out a hand to stop the sway of the cushioned seat, wishing she could sit down and try it out. Because she dreaded facing Benjamin/Ethan. Or whatever his name was.

Her face burned with mortification at the memory of the man seeing her in the bathtub. At least she'd been mostly covered by soap bubbles, desperate to tear the entire shower curtain over the top of her head.

Allie's heart hammered in her throat.

Mr. Miles the Third owed her. Big time.

Even *if* Viola Stark had already promised a rent-free summer.

Fatigue sagged at her after the long, hot day at the fry shack. She wasn't used to long hot days standing on her feet after two years in an air-conditioned office.

Quietly closing the front door, Allie began to tiptoe up the stairs. Halfway up, she paused to speak in a firm voice, deciding it was better not to mince words. "I don't care who you are, Mr. Miles, if you own the house or not, but if you aren't out of this house in two minutes I'm calling the police."

He materialized out of the darkness, flipping on the lamp sitting on the foyer table. "I'm sorry, but we have a problem."

Allie gave a brusque laugh. "No, *we* don't. *You* have a problem. I rented the house for the summer and you have to leave. And not come back until after I return to Toronto."

He cocked his head. "Toronto? I thought you were a native Heartland Cove citizen. Your family owns the fry shack—which has been around since I was a kid."

"Yes, I was born and raised here, but I went to school in Toronto and have been living there for seven years now. I'm only home to help my parents out."

He frowned again. "Nobody would quit a good Toronto job to sling fries for a couple months."

"I didn't quit—"

"I'm sorry if you were laid off. The economy's been bad everywhere." A tone of sympathy warmed his voice and Allie couldn't tell if he made her feel better, or just more irritated.

"I do not want to talk to you," she reiterated. "Please leave. Please."

"Well, that's the problem," he said apologetically. "This is actually my house. My grandmother gave it to me. And I came home for the summer, too. Somehow Viola didn't get the message. Or lost it. Or . . ." his voice trailed off. Meaning it wasn't his fault. Or Viola Stark wasn't particularly organized.

Allie blinked at him. "I paid for this house under a good-faith clause that the property was available. You can't kick me out. I had nothing to do with yours and Viola's lack of communication. And I have the law on my side."

"I never said I planned to kick you out."

Allie took two steps down the staircase. It was beginning to annoy her to only see the top half of his head while they talked. "Before this conversation goes any further, would you please hand over a photo ID and the key you employed to gain entrance into the house while I was, um, upstairs?"

He studied her, a quirk of a smile crossing his lips. "Are you a lawyer by chance?"

"No, but my fiancé is a lawyer. My ex-fiancé that is," Allie corrected, and then regretted saying anything at all. Admitting Sean Carter existed made her feel more vulnerable. And, after a strange man had barged in while she was taking a freaking bubble bath, she didn't want to feel any more vulnerable than she already was.

"Aah, I see."

Emotion flared in Allie's chest. "No, you do not *see* anything. Besides, didn't you just get off the tour bus yesterday? That doesn't mesh with you being a Heartland Cove descendant or heir to this house."

He had the good sense to look sheepish. "I, um, just pretended to be with the tour group. I didn't want to bring attention to myself."

"So now you're telling me that you came to Heartland Cove for the sole purpose of consuming Strickland's seasoned fries—" she stopped, afraid it sounded like she was flirting when she was doing anything but.

"Aha! You remembered what kind of fries I ordered."

"What does that have to do with anything? We only serve two kinds. It was a lucky guess." Allie made a noise of irritation. She needed to shut this guy down. "I.D.," she ordered, holding out her hand.

"I'll do that if you hand over your rental lease and check number," he countered, giving her a cheerful wink.

Allie's eyes widened. The nerve! Then she realized that *he* was teasing—or flirting, but she wasn't going to take the time to figure out which one. "*You're* the one that hired Viola to represent this house and rent it out. Go ask her."

He took out his wallet and Allie held her breath when he looked up at her through the waves of his hair. Those eyes were penetrating and disconcerting. Why did he have to be so good-looking? So *nice*. It would have been easier to yell at him and throw him out in handcuffs accompanied by Sergeant Bowman if he'd been a jerk.

When Allie reached over the banister to take his driver's license, their fingers brushed and she suddenly trembled.

Snatching her hand away, Allie's face burned. She was an idiot for appearing so nervous. Besides, she looked a wreck. Stringy wet hair from the bath, her dirty clothes thrown back on, not a smidgen of makeup. Could it get any worse?

She stared at the ID. Yes, it was definitely Benjamin Ethan Miles the III staring back at her, a mischievous glint in those melted chocolate eyes of his. The address listed on his license was the very house she was standing in. Darn it. Viola Stark was right. Which meant Ethan was right, too.

"You've made your point," she said, biting at her lips when his eyes dropped to gaze at her mouth. "Now leave. I have to get up early. Fries wait for no woman," she added, trying to make her voice light, but her voice came out croaking like a demented toad from the river.

"But I can't leave," he countered.

What was the man's problem? He was so darn stubborn!

"It's very easy," Allie said firmly. "You walk out the door, get in your car, and drive away. Now goodnight."

"Not so easy, I'm afraid." He gave her a guilty smile. "The bed & breakfast is full. I'm too tall to sleep in my car. And this *is* my house. I'd planned to be right here the rest of the summer."

Allie stared at him in disbelief. "Doing what?"

"I'm a photographer. I've been hired to take pictures."

"Of what? The bridge? There are probably thousands out there in the world already."

"Nope. I'm here on assignment. To take pictures of—well, the bridge from various angles and times of day—among other things."

"I can't believe I'm hearing this. *I'm* not going back to my parent's house."

"But you could. Your parents do have a room for you."

"That's beside the point." Allie was suddenly very possessive of this house. Her own Victorian dream house. Hers for the summer. So she could obsess and vent to the rooftops and, hopefully, get over Sean Carter.

Maybe look for a new job, too. Despite what she told

everyone else, she wasn't sure she could return to Toronto, knowing she might run into Sean—even though the city had a population of two and a half million. Still, they had mutual friends and favorite restaurants. It would take effort *not* to run into him.

Ethan raised a finger in the air to stop her from yelling at him. He glanced about the living room, his eyes roaming toward the dark kitchen behind him. "I have a proposal."

Allie put a hand on her hip and arched one eyebrow.

His eyes flickered over her hip and then away. "I'm going to suggest that we share the house. It's big enough for both of us. There's a guest room downstairs including its own en-suite bath."

"I already claimed—and unpacked—in the master suite," Allie interjected.

"And you shall have the master suite!" he said, his voice rising like a television announcer. He picked up his suitcase that Allie hadn't noticed sitting near the front picture window, hidden in the folds of the thick draperies.

Allie gulped. He was truly going to stay here. *Here.* In this very house. With her. "You're kidding," she whispered.

He gave her a smile. "I'll take the downstairs and you can have the upstairs. Evenly split."

"What about the kitchen? I have stuff in there already. I need to eat." Allie thought about the five pounds she'd gained during her week of binge-eating grief. Maybe she should actually stop inhaling so many meals for a while.

"And you shall have kitchen privileges," he added.

"So generous, aren't you, Mr. Ethan?" Allie retorted with a huge dose of sarcasm.

"Please call me Ethan, not Mr. Ethan."

"But isn't your surname actually Miles?" Allie asked sweetly.

He grimaced. "A name I've been straddled with my entire life. My great-grandfather's mother had an attachment to that name, but I do not. While I'm here I'm Ethan Smith."

Allie's eyes narrowed. "Smith? So creative. Where did that come from? Viola Stark said you wanted to be incognito this summer, but a pseudonym of Smith portends nefarious activities. Believe me, I shall endeavor to learn why."

He gave her a wickedly good-natured grin. "And I'm sure you shall Miss Strickland."

Holding her head high, Allie ascended the staircase, one hand gripping the banister. The final exchange with Benjamin Ethan Miles/Ethan Smith reminded her of a conversation out of a Jane Austen novel.

Once inside her room, she firmly locked the door.

"What have I done?" Allie muttered after she pulled a clean nightgown over her head and slipped between clean sheets. "I'm sharing a house with a man I thought was a potential rapist an hour ago."

Two seconds later, she threw back the covers and stomped over to the door, double checking that it was locked. Then she took the heaviest Victorian chair from the corner made of scrolled filigree and velvet and stuck it firmly under the door handle. "There, Mr. Ethan Smith. You can go jump off the Heartland Cove Bridge for all I care."

CHAPTER 8

On her lunch break the next day, Allie went to the hardware store and bought rope, a lot of it.

At the local variety store, she purchased several cheap white sheets—flat, not fitted, and good for hanging.

She met up with Marla for sodas at the gas station and brought a bag of hot fries to share. They sat in a couple of cheap plastic chairs in front of the fry shack that overlooked the Saint John River, between the second and third tour bus of the day.

While they ate, Allie dipping her fries into a puddle of vinegar, she told Marla about Mr. Ethan Smith, incognito photographer lurking about town.

"I think I've seen him," Marla said, sipping at her soda.

"And look at this." Allie reached for the morning paper her father had been reading earlier, muttering viciously at the headline.

Mayor Jefferies in Discussions With The Ministry of Transportation. Proposal for New Highway Bypass Voted on Soon.

"You might as well kill off the town," Allie seethed, skimming the article. "They're going to bypass the town? Two hundred years of history will disappear into the hills. Everybody's livelihoods will dry up—the bridge, the tourists, the fishermen—just like that." She snapped her fingers and threw the paper down, kicking it away with her sandaled foot.

Marla swallowed the last thick fry, closing her eyes in salty ecstasy. "It is disturbing, but I didn't think you cared that much for Heartland Cove. We were both so eager to leave town as soon as we graduated, we would have *paid* the mayor to never return."

"It might be a claustrophobic town with annoying tourists who leave trash everywhere and have nothing for teens to do, but it's my hometown. This will devastate my parents. So many families who've been here for generations."

"Hopefully there's a petition and we can get all 899 citizen signatures and shove it in Mayor Jefferies' face." She gave Allie a discerning look. "If I'm not mistaken, I think you're ticked off about more than just political talk and highway shenanigans."

"Not at all. Just the mayor, the bridge, my parents, Sean Carter, Ethan Smith, and *my* house. Well, my new *rented* house," she amended.

"Goodness, girl, smooth out the furrowed brow, please!" Marla said with a laugh. "Maybe we need to have a movie and popcorn night sooner rather than later."

"Soon, please! With chocolate." Allie smiled at her friend, realizing how much she had missed Marla over the last several years away in Toronto.

"So Mr. Ethan Smith," Marla said, returning to the previous subject. "The man is a hunk of the highest order—and I know you won't contradict me on that point, but I also hate him."

"Why do *you* hate him? I'm the one with the hate rights."

"Because he's a professional photographer with some highfalutin' magazine like *National Geographic* and he's going to steal all my new business."

Marla had returned to Heartland Cove hoping to turn her

photography into a full-fledged business and Allie had thought they'd use the Victorian house to get started because it had a good address and was easy to get to from anywhere along the river.

Marla had already made up a flyer and business cards. She hoped to do not only weddings, but family portraits, wedding anniversaries, birthdays, and set up a daily stand at the bridge to snap pictures for either the romantic couples kissing on the bridge—or all those smiling families with their wild, unruly, happy children.

Kissing was a tradition on the Heartland Cove Country Bridge. Practically an institution that dated back to horse-and-buggy days. Couples would furtively pause halfway across the bridge and steal a kiss at a day and age when chaperones were the usual order of courting.

Allie and Marla had been toddlers when the first couple had taken their wedding vows on the bridge. All traffic stopped and the interior of the bridge was packed with family and curious spectators.

Couples came from all over New Brunswick to tie the knot. Marla wanted to capitalize on those marriages too, including traditional weddings in churches.

She and Allie had it all planned out. With Allie's computer skills, she'd do the photo-shopping on the images, pop them into frames and voilà, The Kiss would be born—an instant gift or souvenir.

"I had originally thought we could use the guest suite downstairs in my new—old—house and the closet for a dark room," Allie said. "If you want to do old-fashioned developing." She made a face. "But nooooo, Mr. Ethan Smith, some dude who inherited one of the best Victorian homes in town from his dear old dead granny, just *had* to show up."

"In your bathroom, no less." Marla made a funny face, which set them to giggling as they tried to outdo each other. Face-making was a pastime of their childhood, when they'd been bored to tears all summer. That and blowing the biggest bubbles with pink Bazooka bubble gum.

"My brother has been working on a sign for my photography business," Marla said once they stopped laughing.

"You mean as in literally hang out a shingle?"

Marla widened her eyes. "Of course. Like a real business."

"That's perfect. Have you decided on a name?

"How about Marla's Magical Moments?"

Allie waggled her eyebrows. "Folks might mistake you for an escort service."

"You would think of that, Allie!"

"Well, maybe I'm scarred by my canceled honeymoon. I'm certainly missing my magical moments." There was a pause as Allie's voice choked for a moment. "Good grief, I feel like such a baby crying again."

Marla leaned over to hug her. "Hey, it's going to take time, honey. Give yourself a break. It's barely been a week."

"It will be much easier when I can full-on hate Sean. I'm getting there, but not quite yet."

A flush of intrigue crossed Marla's face. "Don't look now, but Mr. Ethan Smith is in that far thicket of trees and looking mighty fine—but quite furtive, too."

Her best friend's words pricked at Allie in the oddest manner. "I suppose you'd feel a kinship with the guy. Both being photographers and all."

Marla threw her a shrewd glance. "And he's dripping with good looks."

"I suppose if you like tall, dark and handsome men," Allie said casually. "Of course, I don't feel any sort of ownership over the man. Quite the opposite. He's a jerk for making me share the house with him. A car could have been quite comfortable, I think. I should have thrown him a blanket and pillow last night and made him sleep on the porch swing."

"Try that tonight and see what he says because I want to claim his guest bedroom. Tell him I'm your long-lost sister."

"Yeah, like he'll really believe that. Me, a blonde, and you a redhead with highlights."

"Long-lost cousin then?" Marla slipped her arm through the crook of Allie's elbow. "Come on, let's take a little walk."

"Furtive, eh?" Allie rose to her feet, catching sight of Ethan's figure weaving in and out of the trees. "Let's follow him, and then I have to get back to work. But I have a strong suspicion Ethan Smith is up to no good."

"Watch out, citizens of Heartland," Marla said in her radio announcer voice. "Allie Strickland's sleuthing hackles are on full alert." She tossed the two empty drink cups into the trash container. "When does the next bus come?"

"Not for another twenty minutes. Maybe we can follow Ethan along the pedestrian path of the bridge. I haven't had my dose of nostalgia for the Heartland Cove County Largest Bridge in North America in two years. I need to feast my eyes if I'm a native, right?"

"It's in our blood," Marla agreed. "We're made up of the molecules of Heartland Cove County Bridge. We've breathed them in since childhood."

"We must all be related then," a masculine voice said behind Allie's shoulder.

She practically jumped two feet into the air, clutching a hand to her chest.

Ethan Smith crunched through the gravel toward the road, his head dipping under the lower branches of the trees.

"Were you eavesdropping?" Allie demanded.

"It's hard not to when you two women are talking so loud out here in public."

"We're not in public," Allie contradicted. "Marla and I are alone. You're following us."

Ethan shook his head. "Nope, I've been checking out the

sunlight. At different times of day, that is." He squinted up through the canopy of thick pines and held his camera out with stretched arms, making adjustments to the lens aperture.

"There's hardly good light in the shade," Allie pointed out.

Ethan's lips cracked a smile and the next thing she knew he was falling into step with them. Almost immediately he and Marla launched into a discussion about cameras, brands, prices, and the results they gave, including cameras for various seasons of the year, or for shooting different events.

Allie was well acquainted with Marla's camera talk over the years so it was familiar to her, but not particularly riveting. What *did* she find fascinating? She used to find Sean's lips fascinating. Without thinking, she found herself staring at Ethan Smith's attractive mouth and quickly looked away.

She wasn't going to start comparing the two men. There was no point. Ethan Smith had disrupted her desperate need for quiet so she could figure out where she'd gone wrong with Sean. Had she been blind to his true nature, or had there been signs she'd ignored?

Ethan had ruined everything. Why couldn't he just go away?

Allie blinked when she noticed Ethan gazing at her curiously. "What?" she asked. "Do I have ketchup or French fry grease on my face?"

"No, you were just staring daggers at me."

Allie's face flamed. "I was—I was thinking about something else entirely. Sorry."

"You appeared to be having quite an intense conversation in your mind."

"It was nothing. Just daydreaming." Allie desperately tried to think of how to change the subject when the road turned and the river came into full view, the surface sparkling under the afternoon sun.

"So there's the bridge," Ethan said, rocking back on his heels and then taking a stance to snap fifteen shots in a row.

"Yep, there's the bridge," Allie repeated, stating the obvious in a joking manner. "You ever seen it before?" Quickly, she shook her head, waving a hand through the air as if to wash away her stupid words. "Of course, you have. You were here yesterday taking pictures."

"If you recall, I grew up here, too."

"Right, right." Stupid must be her middle name today. She blamed it on the lack of sleep from having a total stranger downstairs, despite having a chair shoved under the doorknob to prevent potential sleepwalking intruders. "Except I don't know you, and everybody in this town knows everybody else. I've never seen you before—until last night."

"I was a few years older than you in school."

"That makes sense," Marla said. "I would have remembered a Miles the *third*—and probably made fun of him."

"Nobody gets to choose their own name, do they?"

"Touché," Marla said.

"My mother used to tell me every day that Benjamin Ethan Miles the Third was a fine and distinguished name."

"So why are you using an alias now?" Allie asked pointedly.

Ethan's eyes hovered behind that beautiful shock of dark hair. It looked so soft she wanted to touch it. Instead, she clenched her fist to keep from embarrassing herself.

"You're bent on catching me out, aren't you, Miss Strickland." It was a statement, not a question.

She widened her eyes innocently. "I wouldn't even be talking to you now if you hadn't barged into my house, Mr. Smith."

"Come on, you can drop the Mr. Smith business. I'm not an old man."

"But you graduated *years* before we did," Allie said, openly smiling now. It was easy to tease him. She gazed out at the slow-moving water, knowing she was punishing him over breaking into her house and scaring her half to death.

Now that she thought about it, Ethan had been just as freaked out as she had been. She put a hand to her hot face. Had he seen anything more than a flurry of towels and a hysterical woman? That aspect of it made her embarrassed to walk alongside him knowing he might have seen way too much of her soapy skin.

Ethan glanced away as if he could tell what she was thinking, almost as if he were just as embarrassed as she was.

At least, he wasn't acting like an obnoxious jerk like some other guy might have. Or making jokes in poor taste. If he'd done that she would have changed the locks on the doors and thrown him out on his rear.

Allie squirmed thinking that Sean would have most likely been the kind of man to joke about it, shaming the poor girl he'd barged in on. Had she been about to marry a man who was actually a jerk deep inside?

Allie gazed past the span of the bridge to the grass and parking lot on the other side. A family was taking pictures.

"Potential customers, Marla," she murmured, poking at her friend.

While they stood for a moment admiring the historic structure, two teenagers, a boy and a girl, appeared out of the marshy area and began to climb the wooden planks of the bridge. The girl's shiny brown hair swung like a sheet of water down her back, her sunglasses perched on her head, while the young man in jeans and t-shirt, helped his girlfriend up the side.

"Oh, gosh," Marla said. "We used to do that all the time, Allie."

"Ssh! It's a secret. Hey, there's the bus. Gotta go. Bye, Marla."

"Goodbye, Allie," Ethan said. "See you at the house later."

"Not unless I get there first and lock you out."

He lifted an eyebrow. "But I have a key."

"You'll have to come up with the secret password if you don't want to sleep on the porch with the dog."

"Hey, when did we get a dog?"

"*We* didn't get a dog. I meant you can sleep on the porch *like* a dog."

Ethan's voice lowered. "Good one, Miss Strickland. I promise I'll be on my best behavior. No chewing the furniture and no pissing behind the potted plants."

Allie pressed her lips together, trying to hold in a choke of laughter. He was clever and quick, but she wasn't going to give him the pleasure of knowing he made her laugh.

"And you can keep it just that, Mr. Smith. Strictly a business deal based on arm-twisting, not mutual agreement. I signed the lease agreement in good faith."

His expression was sober as he glanced across the water. "I think we understand each other. I'll stay out of your way."

Before Allie could say another word, he disappeared up the slope of lawn, retracing his steps to the waterfront road where the post office and the Heartbeat Inn Bed & Breakfast stretched along the river.

"Where do you think he's going?" Marla asked.

Allie shrugged. "To the mayor's office to make a secret deal? To set up his expensive tripod and give the mayor more ammo to ruin the town? I don't know, and I don't care at the moment. But if you hear of a town petition to stop the highway, let me know so I can sign it."

"He's pretty nice, Allie. Don't be too harsh on him. His mistake was innocent, and he's obviously not a vagrant or weirdo."

Allie sighed. "I'll try to be polite, but I can't promise nice."

As she headed back to the fry truck, she was still unsettled inside. Why was Ethan Smith really back in town? Just to take pictures for a magazine assignment, or something more sinister?

CHAPTER 9

By the time Ethan showed up that evening, Allie had finish stringing up the rope and sheets, dividing the front sitting room in half. She moved the couches and chairs so they each had an equal amount of sitting space.

Then she tackled the kitchen. Half the counters. Half the table and half the refrigerator, although Ethan hadn't yet brought home any food. She lovingly gazed at her yogurt, skim milk, boneless chicken breast, and summer grapes, and then proceeded to pull down an ancient-looking Better Homes & Gardens cookbook to look up recipes.

No sooner had she sat down at the table than Ethan showed up with two bags of groceries of his own, and a bouquet of chrysanthemums and daisies.

"Oh," Allie said, pursing her lips as he unloaded them onto the counter, eyeing the flowers suspiciously.

"Am I using the correct half of my space?" he asked.

She nodded, biting at her cheek. "Yes. I just hoped—I mean I thought—you'd be eating out, not cooking."

"I love to cook."

Allie lifted an eyebrow. "Are you trying to annoy me?"

"Would it make any difference in your opinion of me?"

Allie didn't want to answer that. "Can I plead the Fifth?"

Ethan gave a chuckle. He set down a crate of eggs on the counter, and then moved closer.

"Do you have high cholesterol issues from eating that many eggs?" Allie's nerves tingled on high alert at his sudden nearness.

He gave her a mild smile. "May I sit on your side of the table for a moment?"

Allie's eyes traveled up his chest and then to his face, embarrassment making her blush at the way she was admiring his physique. "Um, okay," she said, turning to look out the window.

He straddled a chair and leaned his arms over the back, setting his chin on his fist to gaze at her.

She glanced down at the cookbook, her fingers trembling as she turned the pages without reading them. She was unsure of what his game plan was and why he was sitting so close. "Go ahead and finish unpacking your groceries," she finally snapped. "I'm just looking over chicken recipes."

Ethan reached over and gently closed the book.

At the same moment, Allie tried to stop him and their hands knocked together. She slammed herself back into the chair in an effort to ignore the disarming shivers that raced up her arms and neck, turning her face hot.

Sitting folded her arms over her chest. "Is there a problem?"

"I hope not. I'm officially declaring a truce."

"A truce, eh?"

"Come on, Allie, don't glare at me. I'm perfectly harmless. You can call my grandmother if you'd like. You can ask anyone in town about my reputation and credentials."

"I thought your grandmother was dead."

Ethan leaned back in his chair, shoving his hands into his front pockets while he studied her. "I never said she was dead. I only said she'd given me the house. She decided to let me take possession now instead of waiting until her death. Especially since it's been sitting empty for so long. We hated to see it fall into ruin."

"Ah, I see." Now that she thought about it she realized he was right, but she didn't want to concede his point.

"It's the truth, Allie."

The warmth in his voice when he said her name melted her insides, but she didn't give in yet.

"What's your grandmother's name? You show up claiming all this ancient history in Heartland Cove, but your name and family aren't familiar. Most of us in this rinky-dink town do know each other. Maybe not friends, but at least by sight."

"Well, some of us were totally dorky growing up and stayed in the woods hunting or fishing far from town. Or buried their heads in books and homework."

"I have a hard time believing you weren't the popular kid in high school and voted prom king."

"Nope. I was a true dork. A complete nerd. But you wouldn't know because I'm pretty sure I graduated the year before you reached high school."

"Don't you have any other siblings?"

"I'm the baby of the family. My older sister and brother are married with kids and living in Montreal."

"So . . . grandmother's name is?"

"Elizabeth Stewart. Ellie for short. She's funny and smart as a whip. I hope you get to meet her one day."

"So she's really and truly alive? I've been gone too long and haven't paid much attention to the news of births and deaths here at home."

"She's in an assisted-living center. Due to physical issues, not mental capacity."

"Where are your parents?"

"They're living in Great Britain at the moment, overseeing some international businesses."

"Wow, that sounds fancy."

Allie hadn't meant to be snotty, but Ethan shifted in his chair, obviously uncomfortable with her description of his family.

"I don't want to talk about families. All of that actually makes me a little bit crazy. But about last night—*please* accept my apologies. If I'd had any idea who had stolen into the house—"

"I didn't steal into the house!"

He held up his hands, rocking back in his seat as he realized that he'd blown it again. "Sorry! Bad choice of words. I only meant that when I first came inside I thought I had vagrants here or someone had broken in looking for valuables. I had no clue a woman was here. An innocent, legitimate, and,"—he paused—"very beautiful woman."

"Don't try to butter me up, Mr. Smith."

"I'm not. I'm sure I scared the living heck out of you."

"Thank you for backing out of the bathroom so quickly," Allie conceded.

He leaned over the chair, his chin in his fists as he gazed at her. "Wow, I think I might be making a tiny bit of progress here."

"Don't get your hopes up yet. I may still put you in the doghouse."

"At least I'll be out of the rain."

Allie stuffed back a laugh.

"It's okay to laugh, Miss Strickland."

"I haven't had much to laugh about the past week."

Ethan frowned. "Your family—are they all right? That was your mother last night, right? With the blueberry cake? You know I smelled it all night long, but I was a good boy and didn't steal a piece."

Allie felt herself blush. "Go ahead and have a piece. Have two! I just—I was still in shock and didn't feel like being hostess and serving cake—"

"I'm teasing you. But if you insist." Ethan jumped up and cut a piece from the cake pan, eating the slice with his fingers over the sink where crumbs dropped.

"You're spoiling your dinner by eating dessert first."

He shook his head as he popped the last blueberry into his mouth and chewed, gazing at her with those eyes. Allie felt her limbs go weak. Dang, those eyes were killing her!

"I have this amazing talent where I can eat dessert before and after dinner with no ill effects whatsoever."

A laugh escaped Allie, but she stopped, not wanting to make small talk with this guy, determined to hang onto her exasperation.

In a gentler tone, Ethan said, "And to help you get over the indignation of me barging into your bathroom last night, I brought flowers to help with my desire to declare a truce. I hope you'll accept another apology and forgive me."

"You don't barge into a strange woman's bath and then bring her flowers. It's—it's unseemly."

Ethan opened up the cupboards until he found a ceramic vase and put the bouquet into it, then ran water to fill it up.

Allie stared at him as he placed the flowers in the center of the kitchen table.

"It's been a long time since this dining room table got flowers," Ethan said. "So I'm giving them to the table—the house—and you can just ignore them. And by the way, just ignore the fact that we're neighbors."

"We are *not* neighbors!" Allie spit out.

"Would you rather be roommates?"

"No! Just—shut up, okay?"

He laughed and his voice was warm and deep and sexy. "Consider me the downstairs neighbor and I'll call you the upstairs neighbor. Just don't play loud music after midnight, please."

Allie growled at him, wanting to stay mad, but also trying not to laugh.

"So," Ethan said, leaning back against the sink. He looked so relaxed, while Allie was wound up tight as a corkscrew. "Is there some sort of crisis going on with your family? I can tell that you're distraught about something, and it's not *all* my fault."

"I really don't want to talk about it." Allie rose to her feet. "I'm starving and don't feel like cooking anymore. I think I'll head down Main and see what the special is at Sal's Diner."

Ethan pointed at the grocery bags he'd just hauled in. "No need to go out. I bought fresh lobster at the marina. And the grocer had some good steaks on sale. I'm grilling."

"Is there a grill here?"

"Of course. The house may be old, but we have the most modern amenities. A gas grill of the finest brand."

"Oh, Sears Kenmore?"

"Nope, a genuine Jenn-Air all the way from Fredericton."

"Oh, my," she said smartly. "A man who cooks. I can't argue with that." Actually, the thought made Allie salivate. Lobster and steak on the grill? Cooked by a man? Sean wouldn't have touched an appliance to save his life.

Ethan headed back out to his car, and unloaded the final two bags which included ingredients for a fresh salad and a vinaigrette dressing, as well as breakfast items, bread, lunch meats, and cheese.

"Go ahead and relax," Ethan said, searching the kitchen drawers for tongs and hot pads. "Take a bath after your long day —I mean, no! *Not* what I meant. I'm sorry. And I meant to tell you that I also bought extra heavy-duty locks for your upstairs doors, okay?"

His face had actually turned red, and now Allie was amused.

"I'm going to change out of my work clothes. Unless you need help reading the directions on how to press the buttons on the grill." Allie gave him her poker face and he laughed.

"Okay, smartie. I got it."

At the doorway, Allie glanced back, watching Ethan run the sink water to clean the lobster tails. She said, "Maybe we can take down the sheet over the kitchen table while we eat."

"It'll be easier to pass the salt and pepper," he agreed.

Allie headed upstairs, knowing she couldn't stay angry forever. And Ethan had apologized nicely. She had needed to hear another apology after the scare last night.

But a sincere, heartfelt apology was something she hadn't received from Sean yet. The hurt stabbed at her chest, and Allie wondered if she could ever get over the pain he'd caused her.

Upstairs, Allie took a quick shower, and changed into fresh slacks and a blue blouse. Fluffing at her hair, she realized that her eye makeup was smudged a bit. She considered fixing it, but decided she was not going to primp for Ethan Smith.

When she returned downstairs, the table was set with old-fashioned china and glass goblets.

"Real cloth napkins?" she exclaimed, impressed. "Is there a washer and dryer on the premises?"

"In the garage. Added to the house when my mother was a teenager."

"That's nice to know," she said. "I already have a stack of work clothes to wash."

"I'll bet it's hard work being in a hot truck and standing over a tub of four-hundred-degree oil."

"I worked there all through my teens until I went to Toronto for university. I got used to it as a kid, but it's harder coming back after seven years away. A lot harder on my feet. My parents are my heroes."

"You'll get used to it again. First week is always the worst."

"First weeks are always the hardest—for anything," Allie said, more to herself than Ethan, but she noticed that he looked at her quizzically, as if trying to puzzle her out.

The last thing she planned on doing was spilling her guts to Ethan about being stood up at the altar.

"Did you miss home while you were away?" he asked, setting down platters of sizzling lobster and a medium rare steak drizzled in a delicious teriyaki sauce. There were even steamed veggies to go with the tossed salad. And separate salad bowls.

Was the guy actually a chef that had pilfered his boss's secret recipes? Maybe he was on the run and masquerading as a photographer.

"No," Allie said simply. "And no fair trying to get any past history info out of me. Not tonight, and probably not ever."

He gave her a tenuous smile. "Aye, aye, Captain Strickland. Try some of the salad. It's already tossed with the vinaigrette."

"Dinner looks amazing, Ethan, thank you." Allie cut up her lobster and then a piece of the steak and stuck them in her mouth at the same time. The tender meat practically melted on her tongue. "Oh, wow," Allie moaned. "This tastes amazing. Sean never would have dreamed of cooking—" She stopped herself and choked, quickly gulping at her water.

Ethan heard her, she knew he did, but he had the grace to pretend she hadn't spoken. He was curious, all right, but Allie went on eating as though she hadn't said anything either. She focused on the meal—real food—instead of junk food—that she hadn't had in days.

"Speaking of the fry shack, I get my share of oil burns," she said, covering up the quiet of the dining room. "Got one today rescuing a basket of fries while my mother took care of a customer's complaint."

"Where's the burn?"

"On the side of my palm." Allie held up her hand. "After lots of ice this afternoon it's not bothering me too much anymore."

"Be sure you apply Neosporin to make sure it doesn't get infected. I have some if you need it."

"You certainly travel well prepared."

They ate in silence for a while and then the phone rang.

Allie looked up, startled. "You had the house phone connected?"

"It was never disconnected," Ethan said. "Probably somebody local calling. Nobody around here has my cell number."

He answered it, turning his back to the window to look into the rear yard. Was that a hint that he didn't want Allie to listen in to the phone call, or merely a casual appraisal of the state of the garden?

It quickly became apparent who was calling. Allie stared at the back of his shirt, pretending to continue eating her dinner. Why would Mayor Jefferies be calling Ethan Smith? He was merely a town resident recently returned after at least a decade away . . . somewhere. Now that she thought about it, Allie wasn't sure exactly where Ethan had been living, or where he'd been working for the past decade himself.

"A meeting this coming Monday?" Ethan said into the receiver. "I can make that. What time?"

He listened for another few moments, but Allie couldn't hear what the mayor was saying, even though she stopped chewing so she could hear more clearly.

"Yes, sir. See you next week. Thank you." He hung up the phone and caught Allie watching him.

"I see you there eavesdropping," Ethan teased.

"I'm innocent," she protested. "See? I'm eating," she added with a mouth full. After swallowing, she said, "If your phone conversations are meant to be private, take them in another room."

"Thanks for the advice," he said, pointedly looking at the telephone attached to the wall. It was a 1980s version, of course, with a curling cord. Meaning he couldn't go into another room, unless he pulled half the wall with him.

"That was an incredible dinner," Allie said, taking her empty plate to the sink. "Thank you. I'll wash up since you cooked."

"You don't have to, but thanks. Hey, if you don't mind, I'm going to head out to do a few sunset shots."

"Time is of the essence when taking sunset pictures," Allie called out as he left the kitchen.

A second later the front door closed and Allie rose slowly from the table, her senses on high alert, tempted to follow him and see what he was up to.

She and Ethan were both keeping secrets. But she didn't owe him anything and she supposed that he didn't owe her his life story, either.

Even so, the sheets and rope in the living room were going to stay up—and her room barricaded each night until she knew exactly what Ethan Smith was up to.

CHAPTER 10

Several more days passed and the truce was still in place, although Ethan kept hinting at taking down the rope and sheets. He'd reach up and hang onto the rope lines, hanging there with sad puppy-dog eyes, teasing Allie unmercifully.

He also came and went at odd hours. Allie assumed that meant he was taking advantage of the various shades of light and shadow for photography. But honestly, how many shots of the second-largest covered bridge can you take before your magazine readers were sick of them?

She grew more and more suspicious, especially after the phone call from Mayor Jefferies, so Allie decided to follow the incognito Mr. Smith on Monday morning when he left for his meeting with the mayor, although he never said that's where he was going.

Sure enough, she spotted him entering the city offices before she headed to the fry truck. It was a busy tourist day. Summer was in full swing by now and the weather was perfect. Tourists trampled the scenery and left their trash all over the grass every three hours, despite several conveniently located garbage bins.

In between each tourist bus, the local vendors quickly picked up all the wrappers and trash so that Heartland Cove looked beautiful and pristine. They had a reputation to maintain, after all.

Later that night after work, Ethan didn't breathe a word about his meeting, despite a hundred probing hints from Allie.

"One day," she vowed getting ready for bed. "I will learn what you're hiding, Mr. Smith."

~

Two days later, Marla showed up with news about Ethan. "Since I have more freedom than you do with a new business and very few customers—" she began.

"You think?" Allie asked, cooped up and antsy with nervous energy. It was claustrophobic being in the fry shack day in and day out.

"Do you want me to keep sleuthing on Ethan or have you changed your mind?" Marla asked.

Allie glanced to the other end of the truck where her parents were fixing a sticky cash register drawer. She stuck a crispy fry in her mouth to test the doneness.

Marla grabbed a fry for herself, added salt, and then leaned over the counter while keeping one eye on Mr. and Mrs. Strickland so they didn't overhear their conversation.

Allie put her elbows down and leaned closer, too.

"Here's the scoop," Marla said conspiratorially. "Mayor Jefferies, is definitely holding meetings with contractors and state officials about the highway. He thinks it's going to bring in logging and other revenue. Of course, that revenue won't come to the citizens of Heartland Cove, only the logging companies—and to him from kickbacks from his logging friends."

"And Ethan?"

"He met with them this past Monday. That is a fact. His name was on the meeting minutes. I have a friend at city hall," she confessed with a wink. "But Ethan is up to something else, too."

"What could be worse?"

"I don't know if it's worse, but I followed him into the forest on the other side of town and saw him hard at work gutting the interior of an old, abandoned house."

Allie jerked upright, smacking her head against the customer service window. "Ouch!" She rubbed her scalp. "Why would he be doing that? He's got his grandmother's house. And he's not a construction contractor—he's a friggin' photographer."

"The mystery deepens." Marla lifted her shoulders in a shrug. "I'm only the messenger—and a pretty good spy, I think."

"You're the best. Thank you." Allie chewed on her lip. The truth was disturbing. "How could Ethan be a traitor to his hometown?"

"Money, of course. Like every other land developer. Why is Mayor Jefferies a traitor?"

"Good point. But why would Ethan be renovating some old house if he doesn't intend to live here and doesn't care that Heartland Cove ends up a deserted ghost town?"

"Your guess is as good as mine," Marla said. "What are you going to do?"

The sound of the four o'clock tourist bus coming down the hill razed the air like crickets buzzing. It was a sound Allie had learned to listen for since she was a kid.

Now she shrugged. "Ethan and I are like two cats circling each other. Eating dinner together, having benign chats about our work days, but nothing personal at all. That's because Ethan Smith is some kind of undercover agent for Mayor Jefferies—I just know it. Cashing in on Heartland Cove. I need to hate him despite the heavenly food he cooks."

"I had no idea you'd sell your soul for filet mignon and chocolate mousse, girl."

"I'm cheap that way," Allie said, grinning. "I'm going to have to take a walk on the wild side one of these days and see what I can see," she added, her meaning clear.

"Be careful," Marla warned in a covert whisper. "It may be some super-secret project of Ethan's. Don't approach him. He could get angry if he finds out you've outed him as a government spy."

Allie tried not to giggle, but she couldn't picture Ethan becoming volatile. He was so mild-mannered at the house, funny and charming with a sense of humor. Being a big tease was his M.O, just like her older brother, Jake. And those brown eyes were getting to her more and more, too. But maybe Ethan Smith was just a talented actor, luring her in just to throw her off the scent.

Several more days passed, and, without any spoken agreement, Allie and Ethan had settled into a routine. Ethan did the cooking and Allie did the washing up.

His dinners were heavenly and varied. She could get used to gourmet meals, but all those late-night calories were taking a toll on her waistline so Allie took up running in the mornings before heading to work.

After a breath-taking meal of beef bourguignon and steamed asparagus with hollandaise sauce one Saturday night, Allie pushed back from the table and declared, "I think your photographer persona is a sham. You're actually a trained chef from New York City and running from the Sicilian mob because you stole somebody's recipe box."

His deep brown eyes sparkled and the mesmerizing dimple appeared. "You have a wild imagination, Allie Strickland."

"Prove me wrong," she said now. "Show me your photographs. I haven't seen a single one. Surely, they're downloaded on your laptop. I'm a good Photoshop editor. I could help you as a way to pay you back for all these expensive groceries."

"I refuse any compensation. I cook because I like to come home to a good meal after a day tramping around the world."

"No fair that you get to be outside in this glorious summer weather. That must be how you keep so trim. I'm jealous."

Allie'd had plenty of time to study his athletic build while he was cooking. Tonight, he'd been doing a few sexy dance moves to the old-fashioned radio perched in the windowsill. She'd had to finally leave the room because watching him made her emotionally and physically crazy.

Allie rinsed the dishes and started up the dishwasher. "Shall we retire to the drawing room, Mr. Cook?"

Ethan shook his head at the mocking names she called him, laughing under his breath. "Cooks are never allowed in the main rooms of the house."

"I'll make an exception this evening." Allie tucked her feet up onto the couch. "If you're a world renowned photographer, surely you'd want to show them off."

"I'm hardly world renowned. If I'm a famous photographer then you're a World Master at crispy fries."

"Hey, I resent that! I *am* a world master of fries. And I have the greasy shirts and aprons to prove it."

Ethan laughed just as a knock came at the front door. Her sister Erin poked her head around the doorjamb.

"Hey, Allie, can I borrow your dress with the—" she broke off and stared at Ethan who was lounging on one of the armchairs while her older sister kicked back on one of the Victorian couches.

A blue sheet wavered between them as they talked.

Erin backed up against the wall. "Have I interrupted something kinky?"

Allie quickly sat up. "Of course not. Where is your mind, Erin—in the gutter?"

Her sixteen-year-old sister stuck out her hip. "Who hangs sheets from their chandeliers?"

Ethan jumped up to introduce himself. "It was a purely scientific experiment on not making eye contact when in deep philosophical discussion," he told her trying to hide a grin. "I'm Ethan Smith, nice to meet you, Erin."

Her eyes narrowed, glancing between him and Allie. Without a word, she raced in and out of the downstairs rooms, from the kitchen to the small side sitting room to the rear guest suite—where Ethan's belongings were clearly unpacked and comfortably at home: underwear on the floor, shaving gear on the bathroom counter, and body wash in the shower.

She marched back into the front room. Her eyes bugged out of her head. "You're living with this guy, Allie?"

"No!" Allie protested with a squeak, but her sister continued full steam ahead. "I don't even know this dude, and you've got him living here! And you're like, lying here on the couch, all casual and sexy."

"Hardly—" Allie began, but Erin kept talking.

"And what about Sean your husband?"

"Husband?" Ethan choked out. He spun around, almost falling into the open fireplace as if she'd knocked him over. "You're married? What the heck is going on?"

"Nothing is going on!" Allie burst out. "Be quiet, Erin."

"But where's Sean?" Erin asked again.

"I have no idea, little sister," she hissed. *"And why don't you shut up already!"*

"If Sean knew you were living with this dude he'd punch Ethans' lights out. Two weeks after the wedding and you move in with a stranger. Mom and Dad are going to throw a fit."

"I'm going to throw a fit if you don't shut it, Erin!" Allie took a step toward her, ready to clap her palm over her little sister's mouth.

"Two weeks after the wedding?" Ethan said. "Wow. I can see why you didn't want to talk about your personal life, but I don't intend to get ripped into shreds by your husband. Sean, whatever his name is."

"Carter. Sean Carter." Allie shook her head, growling under

her breath. "His name doesn't matter because I'm *not* married. I'm single. Completely, utterly, irrevocably single. Are you satisfied?"

"So your sister is the one who's unhinged?"

"No, she's perfectly sane, just annoying."

Erin huffed. "I'm *so* telling Mom and Dad that you're living with some strange guy."

"He's not strange." Allie glanced up at Ethan with her own coy grin. "At least not too much."

"This just gets even better," Ethan said. "Now *I'm* the weirdo."

"Are *you* calling *me* weird?"

"You know perfectly well I'm not," Ethan said.

Allie knew she was digging herself a deeper hole with every sentence, but she couldn't stop herself. "No, I don't. You're the one with a fake identity. You're the one sneaking around taking pictures of Heartland Cove so the mayor can bulldoze in his new highway and ruin the town."

Her words about the highway brought Ethan up short. He stared hard at her, moving closer, his masculine scent overpowering her. "Okay, let's get a couple things straight right now. I'll tell you what's going on with me and the mayor, right after you tell me about Sean Carter, your husband."

Allie's face flamed, the room suddenly hot. Black spots made specks across her eyes and then her knees bumped into the edge of the sofa as she tried to rise.

Erin was soaking up every single word, listening to them talk about fake names and non-existent husbands, and a bulldozed town. Not to mention the air was buzzing with this strange electricity that was going on between her and Ethan. There were moments it felt so strong, she swore it could power all the light bulbs in the house.

"Thank you for the information, Erin," Allie said firmly. "But it's time to go!"

Ignoring the command, Erin dropped herself into an

armchair, staring at them with delight. "Wow, this is good. Just keep going. I only wish I had some popcorn."

"Very funny, now leave, please."

"But I wanted to borrow a dress."

"Do you have to do that right now?"

"Yes, I do. This exact moment."

"You are an inflexible pit bull."

"Why, thank you." Sweetness dripped from every word as Erin leaned back into the chair, as if she planned to stay all night.

"Go upstairs and raid my closet," Allie finally ordered, pointing a finger at the stairs. "You have ten minutes. Go!"

"Will I know which bedroom is yours and which is Ethan's?"

"There won't be a single doubt in your mind, dear sister."

She and Ethan watched Erin move slowly up each stair step, sliding her fingers along the banister as she taunted them with a wicked smile. Finally, she was out of sight and Allie heard the bedroom door close.

"Is she like that all the time?" Ethan asked, shaking his head and trying not to laugh.

"She's sixteen so the answer is yes. All the time."

Allie tried to step away from Ethan, but she'd run out of backing-up space, her legs hitting the couch again.

Ethan was getting under her skin. He made her nervous, excited, like she was on fire and would explode any second if he looked at her one more time with that face, that smile.

She should have stayed in Toronto and faced Sean and had the big, ugly fight. The last two weeks had smacked her in the face with reality. She'd been pretending everything was okay, and it was not okay.

Her entire life was a farce. A lie. One big ball of sorrow and pain and regret. She'd been hiding here in Heartland Cove. Lying to her family and herself. Terrified every single day that Sean was going to call and want her back.

What terrified her most was that if he did show up, she might actually return to Toronto with him. Which meant giving up any self-respect she was slowly getting back if she allowed Sean to take charge of her life again.

She'd wanted him to love her, and when he hadn't, she'd been aimless. A hollow mess of a woman.

With a sudden whisper, the magazine she'd been flipping through earlier in the evening slowly slipped from the velvet couch and hit the floor.

Ethan reached down and picked up the magazine, gently placing it on a side table. With every step, he got closer and closer, his charismatic presence powerful and magnetic, making Allie waver on her feet.

She tightened her fists to her sides to keep from falling into his arms, fearing her heart would explode out of her chest it was pounding so loud.

CHAPTER 11

Holding Allie's eyes with his, Ethan softly said, "So you were about to tell me all about your mystery husband before Erin showed up."

"You mean you want the truth?" Allie croaked.

"That would be a good start."

She waited for the recriminations and accusations, but instead, Ethan gave her a devastating smile filled with real empathy. It was beautiful and charming, and Allie melted despite her effort to remain in charge of the conversation.

"I—I can't, Ethan," she finally admitted. "It's too hard to talk about."

His eyes latched onto hers like a lifeline. His aftershave was killing her, and she wavered again on trembling legs.

"Come on, Allie, talk to me. You're hurting. I can tell you've been carrying something difficult and sad inside you ever since I met you. It's in your eyes and your words, and the pensive way you stare out the windows every night."

"Just my reaction to a potential burglar," she tried to deflect, but her laugh was shaky, and he probably knew she was lying again.

"Tell me," he said quietly. "Quit carrying the burden alone."

"How can I possibly explain the worst day of my life?"

Ethan's brows drew together. Briefly his hand touched hers, and then dropped back to his side. "What did this Sean guy do to you?" he said, and his voice was so gentle, Allie's eyes filled with tears.

She tried to turn away, desperately blinking away the emotion welling up inside of her, but a tear slipped out and rolled down her face.

Ethan reached out to touch her cheek, his thumb soft on her skin when he smoothed the tear away.

"We've been sharing dinners and rooms divided with cheap sheets for almost two weeks now," Ethan went on. "I'll keep any confidences, but I can tell you're about to break apart with some kind of grief. Did your husband die?"

Allie was sure she'd choke on the lump in her throat. "Are you now going to tell me that you have a degree in therapy or counseling?

"No, but my friends tell me I'm a pretty good listener."

"They do, eh?" Her small-town accent came through suddenly, thick and transparent. Allie tried to turn away again to hide her emotions, but Ethan stopped her.

His warm hand was on her arm. "No hiding from me any longer. We're going to be straight with each other."

She faced him, pleading, "I told you it was better if you just left. I really need to be alone. I have so many things to sort through."

"Guess I'm as stubborn as you are," he said.

They stared at each other for a full minute and finally, Ethan's expression softened. "I want to be your friend, Allie. I like you. Does your family know this secret you're keeping? Does Marla?"

She gave a sharp laugh. "They all witnessed the devastation in real time."

Ethan pressed his lips together. "You really are married, then?"

She shook her head and brushed away the fresh tears threatening to spill over. "Dear God in heaven, I want to stop crying. I feel so stupid, so weak. If you must know, Sean Carter was my fiancé. We were to be married two weeks ago—and he left me at the altar."

Ethan let out a low whistle. "Wow, that's a horrible thing to go through. I want to beat up this Sean Carter and I don't even know him. But,"—he paused— "no wonder you hate me."

"I don't hate you, Ethan. Honestly, I don't. At least not anymore."

He gave a laugh and shook his head at her honesty. "Then what can I do for you?"

Allie wiped at her nose. "Just keep making me dinner. I can't seem to focus on anything but slinging fries and crawling into bed every night."

"You got it. Where is this Sean character now?"

Irrationally, Allie's hackles rose at the way he said Sean's name. She realized Ethan spoke only in defense of her, but the whole left-at-the-altar scenario made her feel stupid as if she could have prevented the entire debacle. If *she* had been more worthy, more *something* it never would have happened.

"I have no idea where he is. He texted a few times during the first week after I came back to Heartland, but Toronto is over a thousand kilometers from here and he's working on a big case so . . ." her voice trailed away.

"You mean you haven't seen him once since the day you were supposed to get married?"

"Nope, not even for five minutes," Allie said bluntly. "The last time I saw him was the day before the wedding. You know, the whole thing about the groom not seeing the bride until you meet at the church altar."

"A big church wedding, then?" Ethan asked quietly.

"He apologized by text message."

Ethan's face darkened. He looked like he wanted to punch the wall. Allie figured he probably could with those muscles, but the walls of this old house were probably paper-thin, too.

"Don't bother getting angry on my behalf. Obviously, I'm not capable of hanging onto my man."

Ethan reached out to snatch her hand, bringing her close. Their faces were only three inches apart and she could feel his warm breath on her skin. She wavered, fighting the growing attraction she was feeling toward this man.

"That is so wrong it hurts to hear you say it. Sean Carter is the one with a problem. He's an idiot and a jerk. You never deserve that. No woman does."

"I—I was just going for the self-deprecating joke."

"It didn't work, Allie," Ethan said. His tone was so serious Allie felt shivers running up and down her neck.

"Your ex-fiancé has no clue what he missed out on—and I hope he never finds out."

Allie gave a sharp intake of air. "What's that supposed to mean?"

Ethan backed away and Allie almost stopped him, wanting to pull him close again. "I don't like it when women blame themselves when their boyfriend or husband, or whomever, treats them like they're worthless. You're smart, Allie—and funny when you're not trying to be so serious. And, you're beautiful. You really are, but I don't think you have a clue about how you affect me—men, I mean."

His voice grew softer and he lifted his hand, as if he wanted to touch her face, but pulled back at the last second.

Allie became self-conscious at the turn their conversation had taken. And she certainly didn't want to betray that she could have described Ethan Smith using the exact same words.

She couldn't get attached to him. It was too soon, too risky. Besides, she still missed Sean, more than she wanted to admit.

She'd spent five years of her life with him. His rejection had shredded any sense of self she'd had. And it was becoming obvious she had used Sean to build herself up. She'd been way too submissive, letting him call all the shots and run their lives.

"You're keeping secrets from me, too," she reminded Ethan. "I'm having a hard time trusting you with those phone calls and meetings with the mayor. If you're getting ready to bring down my hometown, I'll take you down with it. I'll fight you—I swear I will—"

"Whoa," he said. "Slow down, you're jumping to conclusions, sweetheart."

"Don't call me sweetheart," Allie said glaring at him.

"You're right." Ethan's face fell. "That was patronizing and I apologize. Please forgive me, Allie."

Allie's throat constricted. Ethan was so different from Sean. She had never heard Sean apologize about anything over all the years they'd been together. He was always too busy, in a rush, stressed, over-worked. He had an excuse of some sort every single time—until Allie gave up had given up expecting any sort of courtesy.

Everybody had to brush off some things in a relationship, right? Nobody was perfect. Until Sean did the unforgivable.

So why did Allie still miss him? Why did she lay in bed at night and contemplate taking him back if Sean begged for forgiveness? Was it because she was a sucker—or because she truly loved him and thought he was "the one"?

Those were questions she couldn't answer, not until time passed, or Sean actually showed up on her doorstep. But she wasn't holding her breath.

"I'll tell you everything you want to know, Allie. I'm sorry I've been secretive. Two weeks ago, I didn't know you at all, and I couldn't afford you accidentally leaking what I was doing here."

"If I didn't suspect you before, now I *really* think you're some kind of spy." Allie gave a tight laugh, hoping Ethan wasn't doing something illegal.

The look in Ethan's eyes was downright mischievous. "Actually, I am a spy," he whispered.

Allie clapped her hands over her ears. "Please, no! Don't tell me that. I can't even pick accidental roommates right! This is all a con, isn't it? You're running from the law. You're swindling the mayor. You never grew up here at all. It's all a lie, right?"

Ethan took her by the shoulders, his hands firm and warm. "I'm trying to tell you something, Allie."

Her eyes lingered over the day's stubble on his jaw line. The way his hair curled at his neck, the crispness of his ironed shirt, the smell of his aftershave—it was all overwhelming. She wished she could break his gaze because his eyes really did a number on her.

"Okay, talk," Allie said with as firm a tone as she could muster.

Ethan slid his hands along her arms and down to her wrists, taking her fingers in his for a brief moment. "I only said I'm a spy because I'm working undercover for someone on the city council to stop the mayor from pushing this highway bypass through without the necessary votes. He's also selling the proposal to the rest of the council and other prominent citizens in a less than ethical way. Leaving out facts, that sort of thing. He's also setting in motion a plan to rig the bidding so that his own construction company gets the job, but under a completely different name."

Allie sank back on her heels and Ethan's hands tightened on hers, as if he were holding her upright. "Wow. So all the corruption rumors are true. What's your role? Why do you care? You're just a roving photographer, here today, gone tomorrow."

Ethan glanced away. "That's not exactly true either."

"Go on," Allie said, preparing herself for the worst.

Ethan's thumb rubbed the skin along her wrist in an effort to soothe her. Allie knew she should pull away, but she couldn't. A peculiar feeling shot straight up her spine, spreading through every nerve of her body.

"My family has been buying up land the past few years in an effort to prevent the modern world from invading the county. To prevent Heartland Cove from becoming a ghost town. To prevent upstarts like Mayor Jefferies from setting into motion something that would damage our town irrevocably."

"So what's all the picture-taking for? Your cover?"

"Nope, it's legit. I *am* taking pictures for a magazine out of the big city for a feature of small town get-aways in New Brunswick and Prince Edward Island, but I'm also taking photos of the mayor's plans on exactly where the highway will be bulldozed through. I hope to get evidence of Jefferies backroom deals, evidence of the homes and property that will be sacrificed to the highway gods."

Slowly, he grinned and Allie cracked a smile of her own at his metaphor. A moment passed and she realized that he was still holding her hands. Slowly she tugged them away, dropping her arms to her sides. Ethan pretended not to notice, but Allie saw a flicker of disappointment in his eyes.

"We're on the same side, Allie," he said, lifting her chin with his finger so her eyes would meet his. He wanted her to believe him. "Two weeks ago, I didn't know whether I could trust you. But now I know how much Heartland Cove means to your family."

"I suppose your family risks losing a lot, too, if you've been buying land and property."

Ethan hesitated and Allie's radar warned her that his next words might not be completely upfront. "I don't really want to talk about that aspect right now. I'd rather show you, actually."

"Show me what? If you trust me, just tell me."

"First of all, do you want to meet my grandmother, Ellie? I think she'd love you."

"Wow, that question came out of the blue." Allie paused. "Okay, but I'll meet her on the condition that we're friends."

"Of course we're friends. I hope we're friends. I think you're pretty amazing, actually."

"Just friends, Ethan. That's how it has to be right now. Trust *me*."

Ethan nodded slowly, not exactly thrilled, but not fighting her. "This weekend," he said.

Allie nodded. "Okay. This weekend."

CHAPTER 12

Allie's sister, Erin, immediately spilled the beans about Ethan Smith living in the same house Allie was renting. The following day at work Allie found herself defending her honor.

Her mother couldn't seem to understand the mix-up on the lease. That Ethan owned the house and there was nowhere else to stay and the B&B was booked for the entire summer, and the house was so large, and so on and so forth.

"But darling, how does it look to be living with a man? It's unseemly. And immoral."

"I'm not *living* with him. At least, not in the manner you're implying. I know it's crazy, Mom, but I can't kick him out."

"That Viola Stark woman should find another place for you to rent."

"She returned my money and I was already moved in. That's twice I've moved in two weeks, I don't want to pack up again. I know I'm being stubborn, but I love the house and I'm staying."

"But isn't it uncomfortable and horribly awkward to have a man you don't know living so close? Breathing and sleeping and shaving—and all those other things—right there?" Mrs. Strickland closed her eyes and sank into a hard-backed chair under the truck awning.

"Ethan is downstairs and I'm upstairs and we hardly see each other." The last part was a distortion of the truth since they ate meals together, but her parents didn't need to know that. "Did Erin tell you about the sheets?"

Horror flashed over her mother's face. "Sheets! What are you talking about?"

Allie wanted to throttle her younger sister. "I put up sheets to divide the rooms up. Honestly, don't fret about it. I still have my virtue."

"If you say so, honey." Her mother gave her the "Mom" eye and added, "You could always move back home, you know, and leave this Ethan fellow to his house. Don't you feel it might be impolite to stay on when the house belongs to him and his family?"

"We worked it all out and it's fine. I'm even going to meet his grandmother this weekend. I'm getting more interested in the history of Heartland Cove. She's the oldest citizen alive now, did you know that?"

"Do you mean Miss Elizabeth Stewart?"

"The one and only."

"Hmm. I didn't realize your Ethan Smith was related to her."

Perhaps her mother was smarter than Allie gave her credit for. She could see the wheels turning inside that mind of hers.

"It's complicated," Allie said, rolling her eyes at how silly that sounded.

"How are a young man and his grandmother complicated? Do you need to tell me something?"

"No. Forget it, Mom. Please."

"Hmm." That habit of her mother to end an awkward conversation with a noise in her throat to indicate that she didn't quite believe her drove Allie crazy. "By the way, what do you think of Mayor Jefferies?"

"The mayor?" Allie asked, putting on an innocent face. "I don't even know him. I've been gone seven years. Why do you ask?"

"Your father read an editorial last night with the suggestion of having a recall vote on the last election. He's new, you know."

"What do you mean, new?"

"New blood. He's not a native. I always find people who aren't part of the original founders to be suspicious. Plus he's so *young*. No more than twenty-seven or twenty-eight. How does someone barely out of university get elected mayor?"

"We do live in the 21st century, Mom. And I think you have Ethan mixed up with somebody else. His family has been here since the founding of our quaint little town. Almost two hundred years ago."

Mrs. Strickland shook her head. "We've never had any Smiths here, I'm sure of it."

Allie let that one go. It wasn't worth trying to explain, and the secret of Ethan's true identity was one she'd promised to keep. If she told her mother, he might be run out of town or put in the metaphorical stockades in the town square while people threw rotten fruit at him.

"Well, there are lots of rumors and gossip swirling this summer, honey," her mother went on. "I just wish we had a historical society again. Our president died last year at the age of ninety and she wasn't able to do much for the decade before that due to debilitating arthritis. Everybody is so busy with their busy lives and electronics nobody seems to care anymore about their heritage and the importance of knowing one's history."

"People do seem to live for the future instead of the past," Allie mused. "Hey, the first bus is coming down the hill."

"All hands on deck," Allie's father said from the rear of the kitchen.

Late that afternoon, Ethan showed up with a ten-dollar bill and a request for double fries and their largest burger with all the trimmings.

"You've worked up an appetite," Allie observed.

"Hiking the hills of Heartland has that effect."

"Any new views you've discovered?" Allie asked with a sideways glance at her parents.

"There's a city council meeting on Friday. Will you be home for dinner tonight?" he asked.

Allie stuck a finger to her lips to shush him, glancing over at her parents. "It's movie night with Marla. But we're on for Saturday to meet Miss Ellie, right?" She purposely made it sound like she wouldn't be seeing him until then.

"Saturday morning at ten. I'll pick you up."

She lifted an eyebrow. "Good one, Mr. Smith," she said under her breath, stifling laughter at his shenanigans. If anyone were eavesdropping they'd never know he'd be picking her up downstairs at the same address.

Ethan gave a wave and sauntered off, cramming a hot fry in his mouth to make way for the burgeoning line behind him, but Allie figured the two of them probably weren't fooling her father at all.

∼

W*HEN SHE WOKE* up Saturday morning, Allie yawned and stretched, arching her back like a cat after a twelve-hour nap. A calico kitten curling up at her feet would make a perfect addition to this Victorian house.

She parted the lace curtains at the window, basking in the morning sun. She found that she was looking forward to the day and the time off from work. Erin had agreed to take her shift. If only her sister would keep her mouth shut and not poke her nose into Allie's business.

What would Sean think if he knew there was a man sleeping and showering and shaving just below her? Despite that, it wasn't much different than a man living in an apartment house on the floor below.

Except Ethan cooked.

And she could already smell breakfast. Bacon . . . yum.

Allie jumped into the shower and then blew out her unruly hair, leaving it down rather than tying it up in a ponytail which she did on normal workdays. After dressing in jeans, a yellow lace blouse, and sandals, she was ready for the day, and ready to eat.

Trotting downstairs, she jumped the last two steps, feeling like a kid. She'd slept better last night than she had in the past three weeks. No tears, just a good book to banish the shadows of Sean's betrayal.

"Smells divine," she said when she entered the kitchen.

Ethan turned to smile at her. "You look great," he burst out, his eyes skimming over her with appreciation before he reluctantly returned his attention to the waffle iron.

Allie felt a skip in her stomach. It was nice to be admired, and it was also very nice to feel no pressure, just camaraderie turning into a friendship she would never have expected.

It was easy to be with Ethan—at least when they weren't arguing over life or Heartland Cove and the darn highway. She pictured bulldozers tearing up the lawns, the roads, maybe demolishing an old Victorian here, a modest family home there.

Frustration rose in her chest so she focused on the sunlight streaming in through the french doors that led to the back garden and then gazed at the table which was already set with china and napkins and tea cups.

Syrup was steaming in a pitcher, the butter was soft, and a platter of hot bacon was ready to be devoured.

"How'd you learn to cook so well?" Allie asked, closing her eyes in ecstasy at the first bite of waffles smothered in strawberries and whipped cream. "You should patent this," she added. "Seriously."

"My grandmother," Ethan said simply. "She partly raised me. My mother had to work a lot."

Curious as to what had happened to Ethan's father, Allie started to ask questions but then closed her mouth when Ethan jumped up from the table to retrieve the next waffle, ending the conversation when he began to muse about fixing up the yard.

"If you had unlimited resources, what kind of a garden would you install?" he asked.

Allie set down her fork. "Gosh, let me think. I love wildflowers and benches and a swing and fruit trees and maybe a gazebo."

"That didn't take long to think through," Ethan teased. "But excellent choices."

"An old-fashioned flower garden to go with a Victorian house would be perfect. But it would take a full-time gardener to weed and fertilize. I've lived in apartments the last seven years and have a brown thumb."

"Not even house plants?"

"I kill them almost instantly," Allie said laughing at herself. "One of these days I'll have my own home and gardener, just you wait."

"I believe you."

The kitchen nook went quiet while they finished eating, and then Allie rose to clear the table. Ethan's eyes were on her face. She wondered what he was thinking, but didn't want to ask. There were moments she felt horribly self-conscious around him.

Allie glanced over at him. "Do I have bacon grease dripping down my chin?"

Ethan shook the hair out of his eyes. "I didn't mean to stare, just noticing the sun on your hair through the window. You have a few reddish tints when you turn your head just right."

"You mean I get to be a blonde *and* a redhead?" she joked, setting the dishes into the sink.

"Hey, I'll do those later," Ethan told her. "We've got a date to see Miss Elizabeth Stewart in half an hour. I spoke with her secretary."

Allie let out a startled cough. "Your grandmother has a secretary?"

Ethan gave her a wink. "Oh, I didn't tell you? Sorry, I got distracted admiring my stunning roommate."

Allie stuck her non-soapy hand on her hip. "Keep that up, buddy, and I'll be kicking you out into the yard in a tent, pronto."

"Sorry." Ethan had the sense to look remorseful, and then his tone turned businesslike. "Miss Ellie has a couple of people who help her out and keep a calendar, that sort of thing. Hey, I'll drive. Just grab what you need and I'll meet you outside."

Allie quickly cleared the table and made sure the milk was back in the fridge before retrieving her purse and locking the front door. Was it a good idea that she meet his grandmother in person? It had the appearance of a serious relationship between the two of them—which she didn't intend at all.

At the same time, Allie couldn't stop the jump that rose in her stomach every time Ethan's eyes followed her across a room. The smiles he gave her were shiver-inducing, and those warm chocolate eyes were delicious.

Last night they'd done the dishes together, hands brushing, arms bumping and Allie thought she might come unglued by her attraction to him.

She *couldn't* fall for Ethan Smith or Whatever His Real Name Was. It almost felt like a betrayal to her ex-fiancé, but perhaps that was only due to the many years she'd spent with Sean. It was like they'd already been married—but without the benefits of a shared bed or checking account; vacations, and a hundred other things.

Sudden tears burned behind Allie's eyes as she strode down the driveway toward Ethan's BMW. Sean's rejection still hurt like a thousand needles driven into her heart.

"You okay?" Ethan asked when she slid into the passenger's seat. He reached out to touch her hand, solicitous, intuitive. So much more than Sean had ever been.

"Fine, perfectly fine," she said, blinking back the exasperating emotion. "So where are we going?"

"Miss Ellie lives in the next county. We're going to drive through Musquash Bridge on the way."

"Ah, Heartland Cove's bridge rival. Gosh, I haven't been to Musquash in years."

Ethan's cell phone rang. He answered and listened for a moment. "Of course," he replied. "Right. Tell her we'll see her in a couple of hours or so."

"What's up?" Allie asked when he clicked off his phone.

"Grandmother's caretaker, Helen, says she had a slow morning getting up so she asked if we'd come a little later than planned."

"Oh, poor thing."

"Believe me, my grandmother is anything but a poor thing. Yes, she's getting elderly, well into her eighties, but she's a spitfire and still runs her household."

It was Allie's turn to be puzzled. "Household? I thought she was in a nursing home."

Ethan's smile turned a little bit guilty. "You'll understand when we get there." Quickly, he changed the subject. "Since we already ate breakfast I can't take you out for a meal. Have you been to Hopewell Rocks since you got home?"

"Nope. Too busy standing over the hot fryer."

"What do you say about a bracing walk along the beach?"

"That sounds nice. I could use some fresh air."

"Is that a subtle way of putting down the company you're currently keeping?"

"Don't turn my words upside down!" Allie reached out to give him a light punch on the arm. "Drive, Ethan Smith."

CHAPTER 13

Over the next thirty minutes, Ethan maneuvered the car along winding cliff roads until they reached a flat outcropping and a place to park.

Even though it was Saturday, it was still early enough that not many people were there yet. An SUV was parked further down and Allie spotted an older man along the shoreline below the cliffs, head bent down while he studied a tide pool. The cliffs rising from the ocean floor were stunning and the horizon mesmerizing. It had been too long since she'd seen the sea.

The wind was brisk, but not too wild when Allie climbed out of the car. Without any hesitation, Ethan took Allie's hand in his firm, warm grip and they climbed down onto the golden sandy beach.

"I should have worn runners." Quickly, Allie ripped off her sandals and let the cool damp sand squish between her toes. "When I was a kid, Dad used to bring me here on Sunday afternoons after church, just to get away for a little while when he could sense I was going stir-crazy."

"You have a perceptive father," Ethan said. He tucked her hand into the crook of his elbow and Allie found herself gripping his arm, hyper-aware of his solidness, the heat he exuded, as well as his relaxed, confident demeanor.

Sean Carter was almost never calm. Never content to just *be*. Always talking, always planning, always restless, always on his cell phone, sending texts, updating his calendar.

Several weeks of being away from Sean was giving Allie a new awareness of her life. And the awareness was unsettling, despite the pain he'd caused her and all those sleepless nights and crying jags.

"You okay?" Ethan's voice was soft when he bent his head toward hers.

Allie stared at his profile as if she were coming out of a dreamlike trance. They were facing the ocean now, the tide beginning to roll closer, but not threatening yet.

"You seem a million miles away," he added.

She shook her head. "Just taking inventory of my life, such as it is."

"It's all going to be okay, Allie, I promise."

"How can you make that kind of a promise?"

He shrugged. "Maybe I have the same intuition as your father. I just feel like you're going to be all right. You're stronger than you give yourself credit for. Besides, it's a gorgeous day and I'm very lucky to be with a gorgeous woman for most of it."

"Come on, Ethan, cut it out." But Allie's protest was feeble. This man honestly made her feel better, more tranquil and at peace. Right now, her worries seemed far away, and she couldn't help liking the compliments, too. Sean hadn't given her one in so long she couldn't even remember the last time.

"I don't mean to make you uncomfortable."

"It's not that exactly," Allie tried to explain. "I'm just not used to it, I guess. Been a while."

Ethan's eyes widened. "You were about to get married and you can't remember the last time Sean complimented you—the woman he vowed to love and cherish forever?" He shook his head and Allie could tell he wanted to say more, but was trying to refrain. At last, he burst out, "So the guy is a no-show on the most important day of his life . . . that just proves it all, doesn't it?"

"Please, I can't talk about him. I don't want to think about him. Let's—let's just enjoy the waves."

"I honestly don't want to cause you pain," he added softly.

Allie nodded, appreciating his silence while they finished their walk along the shoreline. She carried her sandals in one hand while Ethan kept her other hand tucked into his arm. It was a gentlemanly gesture, and she loved the feel of his warm strong fingers wrapped around hers.

Why was she so moved by this man—this unexpected, endearing, and kind man?

"The tide is coming in faster," Ethan said. "I didn't check the tide table for today, but we probably have at least a half an hour before this place is ten feet underwater."

Allie didn't want these quiet moment to end. "Guess we'll have to come back to explore the tide pools."

"Let's sit down on those boulders under the cliff overhang for a few minutes."

The wind was turning brisker with the incoming tide. "Wish I'd brought a sweater," Allie said.

Ethan wrapped an arm around her shoulders and brought her closer, shielding her from the breeze.

"I wasn't hinting," she said, making a face.

"I've been looking for an excuse and you gave me one. Well-played, I'd say."

"You're impossible."

"I know," he admitted, but his smile was fading a little.

"What's up, Ethan? I sense that you want to tell me something."

"I hate to spoil this great morning. I was going to tell you after we saw my grandmother, but now . . ." his voice trailed away.

Allie turned sideways to face him straight on. His arm slipped away and she moved closer to capture his body heat, holding down her hair with one hand while it whipped about in the wind.

"Tell. Now," she demanded.

"I need to move out of the house," he said bluntly.

"Oh, wow, I wasn't expecting that." She took a gulp, not wanting to think about him going away if his work in town was done. "Are you leaving Heartland?"

"No—what I meant was that I'm going to try to get a room at the B&B. Or somewhere. Somewhere else, I mean."

"That doesn't make any sense. We already live in our own apartment, me upstairs, and you downstairs."

"No, we don't Allie, and you know it. It's killing me when I hear you cry at night, even though I know you're trying to hide it."

Allie bit at her lips. Maybe those walls were thinner than she'd thought. "Not so much anymore," she said shakily.

Ethan exhaled and glanced out at the ocean before fixing his eyes on hers again. "I hate that he hurt you so deliberately, so cruelly. The truth is, Allie, I'm attracted to you and I'm having a hard time controlling *my* emotions."

A hundred thoughts and emotions swirled inside Allie's mind. She'd been trying to deny it, too.

"Say something, Allie. I'm going crazy here. I can't be at the house all the time or I'll explode with my need to be near you. One of these days I won't be able to stop myself from carrying you up the stairs like Rhett Butler with Scarlett O'Hara."

Ethan tried to make a joke out of it, but Allie sensed that he was serious.

"That's one of my most favorite romantic movies," she said softly, brushing her flyaway hair out of her eyes.

Ethan caught her hands and brought her closer, soaking up her eyes and mouth with a hungry look.

"I—I'm on the rebound," she said, glancing quickly at the

waves crashing along the shoreline. If she kept her gaze fastened to his she'd probably start to swoon. "I'm not to be trusted."

"Feelings or intuition never lie. I think you're beginning to come to grips with the signs about Sean's lack of character."

Allie gulped in air. "How do you know these things? It's like you're inside my head."

"Somehow, you and I are connected. I felt it right away, even when you were threatening to kill me."

Allie gave a quick, sharp laugh. "Isn't that just a bunch of hocus-pocus? 'Feelings', I mean." She put air quotes around the word. "Our feelings confuse us, and then betray us. Every single time."

"Stop talking like that, Allie," Ethan ordered huskily.

Before she could say anything else, his arms went around her and he pulled her against him. She felt his chest and stomach muscles underneath his sweater, his breath spicy and masculine in the most delicious way. He was so close, so handsome, so perfectly the right height, his warm fingers brushing along her cheek.

He came closer—those eyes!—and Allie was frozen, unable to stop him—not wanting to stop him, her mind whirling with his closeness and the intensity of desire crashing through her.

Before she could take another breath, his lips melted against hers, warm and tender and indescribable.

Ethan pulled her arms around his waist as he deepened the kiss. Allie's heart pounded so hard against her ribs she thought she might pass out.

Frothy waves crashed while they sat locked together on the beach in their own little cocoon. Allie lifted her chin, kissing Ethan back, and his lips were so soft, so perfect, she couldn't seem to get enough.

A moment later, Allie sagged against his chest, tugging at his shirt collar with her fingers while she buried her cold face into his pullover sweater.

"You—You—" she tried to speak.

"What?" he whispered, his hands cupping her head to keep her close.

"That wasn't fair. That was—oh, *you*." Allie couldn't explain what she was feeling. Her legs were unsteady, her heart stuttering. Part of her wanted to run—and the other half of her wanted to kiss him all night. In Ethan's arms Allie felt safe. And desired. Because she knew that Ethan only had eyes for her.

Guilt reared its ugly head, though, as she became conscious that she'd kissed another man only three weeks since being left at the altar.

Ethan chuckled at the way she stammered. He placed a finger under her chin and tilted her face up. The connection between them was instant and electric. "I don't care if it's fair or not. That kiss was the best thing I've ever done in my life. I'd kiss you again, but we're drawing an audience on the rock bluff."

Allie shaded her eyes, relieved to see that it was a group of tourists and nobody she knew. She glanced away, not wanting to look at Ethan. She wasn't sure she could take the power of what she read in his face.

"What are you thinking?" he murmured while they gazed out at the white caps growing taller with each passing moment.

"I'm thinking it's dangerous to look at you," she admitted.

His breath was warm against her skin. "Can we take down the sheets dividing up the house?"

"No!" she said vehemently, then laughed at the vigor of her words. "Those sheets are my insurance. Honestly, I don't know what to do with you. . ."

Allie twisted around in his arms, her toes cold and damp as she tried to get her head on straight.

"I was teasing," Ethan told her. "The sheets are not coming down. Ever. Not in a million years. Even if there was a flood, a hurricane, a tornado. Those sheets will remain strung across the house for the rest of our lives."

A giggle burst from her throat, and then Allie glared at him. "You are too much."

He took her hand and tugged her up the path back to the car. "We'd better go now. My grandmother awaits."

They didn't speak again until they were inside with the doors shut and Ethan started up the engine. Before pulling into the road, he turned his head toward her. "If I did something horribly wrong, please forgive me. But honestly, it's all I can do not to kiss you again. I'm going to have a hard time getting your lips out of my mind."

"I'm afraid you're going to have to try," Allie said bluntly in an attempt to get her composure back.

"I felt your heart racing, Allie. Just like mine."

Allie stared out the window. Ethan's kiss was the most tender and sexy kiss she'd ever had in her life, but she wasn't going to tell him that. She couldn't.

One part of her felt like an idiot for ever wanting to marry Sean and the other part of her felt like an idiot for wanting to crawl into bed with Ethan Smith.

It was too fast, too soon. Almost a month ago she'd been practically a married woman, committed to Sean Carter till they parted at death. She couldn't process what was happening with Ethan. Her feelings were crazy, too needy. Maybe that's all this was. She was lonely, vulnerable, and nursing a shattered ego.

At the stop sign, Ethan put on the brake. He glanced down the road but there were no other cars in sight. "Before we continue to my grandmother's place, I have to know one thing."

She frowned. "What's that?"

"Please tell me I'm not crazy," he said. "Tell me if that kiss was the real thing, or not. I need to know one way or the other. I'm not going to pressure you to change our relationship, but I also don't want you placating me or brushing me off. It's important, and you'll soon know why."

Allie stared at him, bewildered. "You are a mystery, Ethan."

He didn't say another word, just waited for her next words.

"Okay," she said at last. "I worry that I'm crazy and needy and silly and need a man to reassure me after what Sean did. That I'm just lonely and desperate." She paused. "But, yes, that was probably the best kiss I've ever had in my life. And yes, I've been attracted to you for at least a week."

"Only a week?" Ethan's laugh was soft. "Oh, Allie, you're something else."

Turning into the road, he reached over, took her hand, and pressed his lips against the back of it without another word.

CHAPTER 14

Ethan didn't try to touch her when they parked the car and walked up the path to the "nursing home".

"This is the nicest nursing home I've ever seen," Allie said, lifting an eyebrow quizzically.

"Well," Ethan confessed, "It used to be a nursing home that was abandoned. The owners of the property were going to demolish it until good old granny bought it, gutted it, and turned it into her own little palace."

Allie looked at him quizzically when the front door opened and a man dressed in a black suit stood on the other side—wearing gold cufflinks and a tie.

At first, Allie thought he might be Ethan's father, but Ethan shook his hand, calling him Mr. Sherman.

Soft orchestral music was playing somewhere, but after a moment Allie realized the music was being piped throughout the house. The furnishings were impeccable. No expense had been spared: flowing draperies, plush couches, thick mauve carpets, parquet flooring, huge paintings on the walls—family portraits mostly, some dating back to the Regency era of the 1820's.

Allie had the oddest sense she was in a replica of one of the manor houses of England.

The place was lavish, but tasteful, and it reeked of money. Obviously, Miss Elizabeth Stewart wasn't just well off, she was flabbergastingly wealthy.

"Is she really your grandmother?" Allie asked in a low voice, wondering if this expedition was some kind of a joke. She tugged at Ethan's sleeve while Mr. Sherman escorted them through the living rooms to the master suite beyond. "Or some rich family friend your mother likes you to visit?"

Ethan raised his eyebrows at her doubts. "Nope, she's my grandmother all right. The one and only."

"None of this is jiving," Allie muttered as Mr. Sherman escorted them into a beautiful sitting room adjoining the master bedroom suite. "And you're just a photographer journalist. Right."

Morning light poured through a wall of windows centered by a pair of french doors which opened onto a stone patio flush with hanging flowers and bordered by roses. Dotted by huge shade trees, an emerald lawn stretched out, so lush Allie wished she was a kid again and could go rolling down the grassy slope to the pond below. She and her brother, Jake, used to roll down the hill at the town park when they were kids.

"What a gorgeous room!" Allie exclaimed, unable to help herself.

An elderly woman's voice spoke to her left, "The remodel *did* turn out nicely, didn't it?"

Allie turned to see Miss Elizabeth Stewart leaning on her cane and gazing out at the beautiful morning. The older woman was wearing a flowing dress with coiffed snowy white hair and blended pink rouge on her cheeks. Her back was straight despite the cane, and her smile genuine.

"I just hope heaven is as nice as this when I die," Miss Ellie went on. "The house and landscaping took over a year to finish—

and when you're eighty-eight years old that feels like half your life."

"Grandmother does everything superbly," Ethan said. "No detail overlooked." He opened the french doors for them to step through onto a sprawling concrete patio that had been stained to look like silver-veined granite. "Shall we?"

"I think I just stepped into a dream," Allie said.

"Why, thank you, my dear," Miss Ellie said. "Sit down, you two. We have this nice table to sit at, and Mr. Sherman is bringing brunch."

Allie opened her mouth to say that they had already eaten breakfast, but Ethan gave her a quick wink and held a finger to his lips. Allie nodded, understanding that he didn't want to hurt his grandmother's feelings by not eating the specially prepared food.

The table was certainly not a picnic table though. Gleaming white wrought-iron, cushions on the chairs, and adorned by a glass top with a basket of fresh flowers in the middle.

No sooner had they sat down than Mr. Sherman poured juice and coffee and laid out scones and jam and clotted cream, as well as an abundant fruit salad with another platter of rolled ham and pastrami.

"This looks beautiful," Allie said.

"Dig in," Ethan added.

After the walk along the shoreline of Hopewell Rock, Allie found that she'd burned off breakfast and her stomach was giving off signs of hunger.

"Cream, Miss Strickland?" the butler asked, bending over to pour from a quaint pitcher

"And sugar," she said, feeling self-conscious when Ethan was having his coffee black. "I have a sweet tooth."

"Give the lady another cinnamon roll," Ethan added.

A plate of warm and gooey cinnamon buns appeared next. "Oh, goodness," Allie said, sniffing in the yeasty smell of rolls and cream cheese frosting. "Remind me not to eat dinner. I think my calorie count has reached its limit already."

"But it was your turn to cook tonight," Ethan teased. "You're just trying to get out of it."

Miss Ellie turned her snapping dark eyes on them. "So it's like that, is it? Young people today have no patience. You must live together and act like you're married—only to break up at the first fight."

Allie's eyes widened. "Oh, no, it's not like that at all! I'm upstairs, Ethan's downstairs, we just cook a few meals now and then. There is nothing between us!"

Ethan's face fell and Allie felt a stab of regret in her chest. She didn't mean to sound so adamant or cruel. She just didn't want his grandmother to get the wrong idea.

"I like you better already, Miss Strickland," Miss Ellie said, patting Allie's hand with frail fingers. "Have some more of those perfect watermelon wedges, my dear."

Ethan glanced up at Allie. "Surely there's friendship?"

Allie softened her tone. "Of course, Ethan."

Ethan went quiet, staring out across the perfect expanse of lawns.

"If I'm not mistaken, you leased my little Victorian town house?" Miss Ellie asked.

Allie nodded. "I did. I love it. But I thought—"

The older woman's hand shook slightly as she lifted her napkin to her mouth. "Ethan owns it now. It was a recent coming-of-age present."

"You mean you just turned twenty-one?" Allie said, unable to stop from teasing.

"Thirty," Ethan answered. "Good old thirty."

"The Stewart family has lived in Heartland Cove for many generations now."

"It's an incredible history and family heritage, Miss Ellie."

"The family trust owns the bridge, actually. And much of the land around town."

"My goodness, that's—" Allie stopped herself as chills ran down her neck at the thought of Ethan's net worth.

Ethan had a peculiar look in his eyes.

Allie pressed her lips together, feeling deceived all over again. "I shall call you Benjamin from now on, Mr. *Benjamin Ethan Miles the third*."

"Oh, I do wish you would, my dear." Miss Ellie took Allie's fingers in hers, pressing them lightly with the fragile strength she had in her birdlike hands, purple with veins, despite the perfectly painted pink fingernails. "This Ethan Smith alias business is just silly."

"Grandmother, you know I couldn't come back to town as your heir. We need to stop the city council from destroying Heartland Cove."

"I understand, but I still don't like it. I wish people were more honest. Lies and subterfuge in politics get worse all the time. Nobody keeps their word."

"I understand exactly what you mean, Miss Ellie," Allie told her. She was thinking of Sean Carter, but she was also thinking of Ethan/Benjamin. At least he had a good reason for pretending to be a photographer to learn Mayor Jefferies' secrets.

"Keep me posted on those meetings," Miss Ellie told her grandson.

"I will. And now I think I need to get Allie home."

"Oh, I'm having a lovely time," Allie contradicted. "I've been waiting to hear all about your childhood, Ethan. Oh, pardon me, Benji."

"You know I hate that name—"

"I know no such thing!" Allie tried not to laugh. It was nice to have the upper hand for once.

"I actually went by Ben as a little kid. You happy now?"

"Deliriously."

His eyes held a touch of amusement, including irony, and then he made another startling confession. "I've actually known you for years, Allie."

"How could you? I'm almost five years younger, which means we didn't even attend high school at the same time."

An expression of mortification crossed his face. "You never saw me, but I saw you. I was in love with the fry truck girl, even though I was just another customer in the long line for the perfect french fry."

No, Allie pleaded with her eyes. "Don't say things you don't mean." Or maybe he did mean them. Which was better—or worse? This man was confusing her.

"Are you going to laugh at the most tender feelings of my youth? The awkward, shy boy who—"

"Oh, shut up. You're pulling my leg now. I can't believe anything you say."

"Allie," he said gently. "I'm not trying to make light of it, but I don't know how to tell you the truth. And, I think you don't want to hear it."

Miss Ellie watched them with great interest. "I feel like I'm inside one of those romantic comedies. Except neither of you are laughing."

Allie put a hand to her cheek, heat flaming her face. "This is so embarrassing. We're arguing like a couple of kids."

Miss Ellie smiled indulgently and shook her head. "No, not like kids. Like two people who—" she stopped abruptly. "Why don't we take a little walk about the property? I need to move, or I'll be glued to this chair forever more. It happens at my age. The doctor gives me this advice: keep eating, keep drinking, and keep walking."

"As long as it's a good scotch, Grandmother," Ethan said with a small laugh.

She swatted his arm, and then ordered, "Let me hold on to you, my dear."

The three of them spent the next fifteen minutes strolling across the lawns and admiring the new windows in the gazebo. Fountains sprayed cool water, misting them as they walked by. Flowers were heady with perfume. Allie felt as though she were swimming in perfect beauty.

Mr. Sherman provided them with ice cold lemonade on a silver tray at the end of their stroll and then Allie and Ethan took their leave.

"I need to get back to work," Ethan told his grandmother. "And Allie keeps a strict daily agenda."

"Daily agenda?" Allie echoed, shaking her head at his exasperating fibs.

A few minutes later, their goodbye's said, Ethan held the car door open for Allie.

Instead of sliding into the front seat, Allie whirled around on her heels, jabbing a finger into Ethan's shoulder. "You liar! Oh, you're just a poor lowly photographer taking photos of quaint, picturesque Heartland Cove. The hometown that you love so much you'd do anything to save it. You're a filthy rich billionaire, for heaven's sake!"

Ethan took a deep breath, staring into her eyes without wavering. "I brought you here because I knew I couldn't keep it from you any longer. And I brought you here because I trust you to keep my secrets safe—at least for now."

"What are your secrets, Ethan Smith?" Allie asked. "Be honest with me or I'll kick you out of the house so fast you won't know what hit you."

"All right, here goes," Ethan began. "My family was one of the original founders of Heartland over two hundred years ago. We actually own many of the businesses here, including the tourist industry. We hire out the management to provide employment."

Allie's mouth dropped open. "You *own* Heartland Cove? Then I'm right. Benjamin Ethan Miles AKA Ethan Smith is stinking filthy rich. Good grief," she added lamely, realizing how bad-mannered it was to bring up the topic of money.

He nodded, searching her face with a look of—what? Embarrassment? Guilt? Or hope? "Yep, you just met Dame Elizabeth Ethan Stewart, the rich widow that keeps Heartland Cove County on the map and running."

Allie crossed her arms over her chest, trying to keep her brain from exploding.

Ethan held up his hands. "But please, I'm not a billionaire!"

"Ha!" Allie scoffed. "When there are too many millions to count it doesn't matter any longer."

"Well, changing the "m" to a "b" would be pretty nice—" he broke off, aware that Allie was seething, and not laughing. He lowered his voice, aware of potential open windows. "Can we drive home and continue this chat at another time?"

Without answering, Allie finally got into the car and slammed the door.

The ride back to the Victorian house was silent and when they arrived, Allie piled out and slammed the car door again, stalking through the front door and then slamming it next.

"Why the charade Ethan—or Ben—or Miles? My gosh, I don't even know if any of those are your true names!"

He stood in the entry hall staring at her. "What charade are you talking about?"

"Taking pictures to prove to the state, or the county, or whomever about what the mayor is doing. Why don't you donate your millions to save Heartland Cove from bankruptcy? You can buy the mayor out. Bribe him—or something," she added ruefully, putting a hand to her mouth when she realized what she'd said.

Ethan shoved his hands into his jeans, a small grin crossing his face. "I'd like to keep my freedom and not go to jail. Not to mention the fact that the money isn't mine."

"When do you get the trust fund?" Allie couldn't help it. She was point blank, firing questions at him.

"Thirty-five, unless Miss Ellie passes away first."

Allie put her hands to her burning cheeks. "Oh my gosh, here you are a billionaire and cooking my breakfast to boot." The last came out in a strangled laugh. Because it *was* funny—in a bizarre way.

Ethan smiled, his mouth quirking up so adorably Allie had this sudden, insane urge to kiss him again. Instead she clenched her fists so she could stay angry.

He shrugged. "Hey, even rich folks gotta eat."

Allie didn't want to be soothed. "Okay. So what's with the house you're gutting on the other side of town?"

He was visibly startled when she said that. "How do you know about that?"

"My friend Marla spotted you. Are you going to tell me that you are also a construction engineer?"

"Well, actually, I am. Sort of."

"You've had a busy decade since high school."

"I worked construction with my uncle during high school and university to pay my way through."

"Why would you need to earn any money if your grandmother is indecently wealthy?" Allie couldn't stop the sarcasm from coming out of her mouth.

She wasn't normally sarcastic and ornery at all. Sean Carter deserting her at the altar and ruining her life had changed her. It was his fault. But Allie knew that was only an excuse. How dare Ethan make her attracted to him and get her all flustered—just before she learned he wasn't who he said he was? How could she trust anyone?

"My grandmother's money is not mine. She gave me this house to fix up, but it was my father's brother who worked construction. My father wasn't the one with the money." He paused, his eyes turning darker than normal, the muscles in his jaw twitching. "My mother never actually inherited Grandmother Ellie's estate. Or took ownership is perhaps a better way to say it. She died in a car accident before her thirty-fifth birthday. When I was ten years old."

Allie's breath caught. "Oh, Ethan, I'm sorry. That was rude of me. I have no business questioning your family's business—or anything. I can't imagine how hard that would be to lose your mother at such a young age."

Ethan touched her shoulder. "There's nothing to forgive. I miss my mother, but I've made peace with it. I also know that I've been secretive about a few things. Maybe it's time to come clean on another project of mine. As in the house in the woods on the far side of town."

Allie watched a surge of emotions cross Ethan's face, and braced herself, hoping he wasn't going to confess to a secret wife and a dozen children in Idaho.

"My grandmother owns that old place, too. And yes, I'm gutting it and remodeling extensively."

There was a pause and when Allie stared into Ethan's eyes she tried not to let her knees go weak. "Will you make me a promise?"

"Of course. Anything."

"Don't lie to me ever again."

"I never wanted to. I hope you know that. But when we first met you were a vagrant living in my house." Ethan said, wagging his eyebrows in a teasing gesture.

"Okay, I'll give you that inch," Allie conceded. "Because you admitted two hours ago at Miss Ellie's house that you've been watching me for more than ten years."

Ethan's face turned red. "Admiring someone from afar and knowing someone personally are two very different things."

"Maybe your opinion of me has changed for the worse. I've been catty and suspicious and irritable for weeks now, and I'm sorry."

"No, my good opinion of you hasn't changed. You've been under a great deal of strain. But you're also holding up admirably given the circumstances."

"Serving our special fries to hundreds of strangers every day will do that to you."

"See?" Ethan's eyes penetrated her thoughts. "You're also funny. Something you don't recognize in yourself."

"Don't look at me like that," Allie ordered. She backed away, seeing too much she couldn't cope with in his face.

He caught her fingers in his and Allie went still, hardly daring to breathe. "You know I'm falling for you, Allie Strickland. Harder than I thought."

"Well, you can't. Because I'm still in love with Sean."

Ethan winced and Allie knew she'd hurt him, but speaking the words didn't make her feel any better. Worse, actually.

He nodded. "You tell yourself that because you're afraid of moving forward. You were with him for so long you can't seem to give up. But he's not coming back. It's been almost a month. It's over."

"Oh, shut up, Ethan Smith."

The pressure on her hand intensified and Allie could hardly take a normal breath.

"You're hanging onto his rejection like a badge of honor. You're comfortable in your pain. And you're afraid so you keep up the pretense in your heart."

She made a face at him like she was still in third grade. "I hate you, Ethan Smith."

He gave a sharp intake of breath. "I understand. I'm sorry for coming down so hard on you and I'll leave you alone now."

But Ethan didn't storm out like she expected him to. His shoulders hunched as he opened the front door and walked back down the sidewalk to his car without another word.

"Don't patronize me, Ethan Smith!" she shouted after him. "You're wrong. You don't know. I can't trust you so just go away and don't come back!"

He stood at the car door watching her for one final agonizing moment. Allie felt like an idiot for the things she'd just said to him. She was so immature. So grouchy and annoying.

Ethan lifted his arm in a brief wave, almost like a salute. He dropped into the driver's seat, banged the door closed, and then roared the engine to life, peeling out of the driveway and spitting gravel.

Allie slammed the front door and marched toward the kitchen, a sob burning at her throat. "Why did you have to show up, Ethan, and make my heart so crazy? Why didn't I kick you out from the very beginning?"

Not half a minute later, the doorbell rang. "Now what?" She stomped back through the hall and threw the front door open again, ready to chew out Ethan for not leaving like he promised.

"Hello, Allie," Sean said, a smile breaking across his face, like a cat that had finally caught the elusive mouse.

Allie felt every last bit of her strength leave. "Sean! What are you doing here—"

"It took me awhile, but I tracked you down. Oh, Allie, I've missed you so much. You won't believe what a crazy month it's been."

Rooted to the floor, Allie tried to take in the fact that the man she'd been about to marry had been searching for her. He was there, standing in front of her like an apparition.

She opened her mouth to speak, but nothing came out. Instead, she sagged against the door frame as her legs turned to jelly.

Just as she was about to crumple to the floor, Sean stepped forward and caught her against his chest.

His arm muscles flexed and tightened, and then he picked her up and walked across the threshold like a groom with his bride.

CHAPTER 15

Sean carried Allie into the front parlor, maneuvering around the furniture. Slowly, he lowered himself onto the settee with its velvet cushions and scrolled woodwork, holding her in his lap.

While his familiar arms were comforting, they were also curiously foreign. After nearly a month apart, it was as if he'd returned as a ghost from her dreams. Almost a stranger in a dozen small ways. Allie noticed the scent of a new aftershave cologne and wasn't sure she liked it.

"What—where—how did you—?" Allie tried to speak but she was incoherent as though waking up from a coma. She'd had a thousand questions churning in her mind for so many weeks, and now nothing would come out.

Before she could form a sane sentence, Sean was bending over her, slipping his fingers through her hair, and then his mouth came down on hers and he was kissing her.

Surprisingly, her own lips softened, and she was kissing him back.

Allie had dreamed about this moment—Sean returning to

rescue her from her mental anguish—so that she couldn't stop herself from giving in to him.

She'd missed him, but after kissing Ethan a few hours ago, his lips were almost like a stranger's.

Sean's kisses were intense, as if he would swallow her whole, his breath ragged as he pulled her underneath him.

She could feel his heart pounding against her chest and Allie couldn't think straight. He was overwhelming her, making her feel wanted, but trapped. His desire was obvious, but she wondered if it was real. What an odd thought.

"I've missed you so much, Allie," he murmured, forcing her lips open.

She gave in, curious as a teenager being french kissed for the first time, but not sure she actually liked how hard his mouth was on hers.

"I've been waiting for that annoying maintenance guy to leave," Sean said, breathing hard as his lips traveled down her neck, going lower and lower.

Gulping in air, Allie pushed at him. "Stop for a moment. I can't breathe. You're overwhelming me."

Sean just smiled while she struggled to sit up. "That's nice to hear. Especially when you stopped answering my text messages."

"*You* stopped texting me two weeks ago," she told him flatly. "And I don't have any maintenance guy here. Who are you talking about?"

"Your landlord must own a bunch of properties if he can afford a BMW."

Finally, Allie understood that he was referencing Ethan. "You saw him? You were waiting out there, watching the house?"

He nodded, running his hand down her arm and then along her waist with a seductive smile. It was a touch that used to send shivers rocketing through her, but now she was getting annoyed at the way he was taking liberties—after no communication in weeks.

Sean had never actually *called* her after his wedding altar no-show. He'd never bothered to speak in person, to explain anything. She was still waiting, and here he was going after her as though they were still engaged—or already married.

"I parked across the street. Didn't you notice my Porsche?"

"You never owned a Porsche." Allie tried to take in the fact that he'd been watching the house. "How long have you been stalking me?"

Sean laughed, finally sitting up. Untangling her legs, Allie tried to slide off his lap, but he held her firmly, stroking her hair, trying to nibble at her ear.

It was really beginning to bother her.

"I'm your fiancé, it's not called stalking when I wait for some plumber to leave so we can be alone. An old house like this, I'll bet it's got a hundred things wrong with it."

"Actually—" she began to speak, but he cut her off.

"Let's just do it, Allie," he said suddenly, his voice turning low and rough. He pulled her close while his fingers fumbled with the buttons on her blouse.

The moment was so surreal. He had three buttons undone before Allie could figure out what to say. Instead, instinct took over. She swung out a hand and slapped him across the face. The sound of the slap bounced off the crown-molding. "What the hell, Sean!"

Surprise swept across his face. "Hey, what's going on?" Then he gave Allie a sheepish expression. "Okay, I guess I deserved that. But now that it's out of your system, let's get married. Find the small-town justice of the peace and make it official. Why wait any longer? This month has about killed me."

"This month has killed *you*?" Allie choked out. She scrambled to her feet, standing over him. "You jerk! *You left me at the altar!*"

"No, I didn't. I called you and told you what was happening. That we just had to have a do-over wedding day. People do it all the time."

"You did *not* call me. You texted me with some stupid story. Listen to me very carefully, Sean Carter, you dense SOB. People do not do-over their wedding day—not when they're already at the church with a hundred guests."

"Isn't it called renewing your vows?" His face was so perfectly innocent and stupid she wanted to slap him again.

Allie's fingers clenched together. She thought she might break off her thumbs. "Please don't tell me you just said that with a straight face. You're a lawyer, are you completely dense? *You deserted me on our wedding day and then you show up here weeks later like nothing's wrong?*"

"But I love you, Allie."

She took a step backward, jerking as if he'd hit her. "Wow. You have a strange idea of what real love is."

"Okay, I'm a jerk lawyer. Guess it comes with the territory. But I'm the same person you've always known, Allie. Nothing changed. I had an emergency and we get married now. It's not like we can't reschedule the honeymoon trip, or send back the wedding silver if that's what you're feeling guilty about."

Allie opened her mouth, but for a moment no words came out. She had no idea where to even begin. "First of all, *I'm* not the one who's guilty. Second of all, being a jerk is something you choose, it's not something you inherit when you graduate from law school."

Sean rose from the couch and she gazed at him defiantly, arms crossed over her chest to keep him at bay.

"I was on the case of my life, Allie. For weeks, I told you it wasn't the right time to have a wedding."

"Pretty hard to start over on wedding planning when we'd already paid the deposit on the church hall, and sent out the invitations!"

Sean squared his shoulders. "I suggested we could live together and do a party some other time when my case load calmed down."

"A party?" Allie spit out. "Our wedding—our life commitment —isn't just some Friday night party so everybody can get drunk. Your case load will never lighten. It will only get worse. Those are just asinine excuses and you know it; you're just too selfish and insensitive to admit it."

Sean began to speak again and Allie shoved a finger into his chest. "Don't play stupid. You made it through law school so I think you can understand what's going on here without playing the victim. You've known that I wanted a real wedding and a real honeymoon ever since we got serious three years ago."

"We can still do it, baby," he said putting on his quiet, smooth voice. "We'll plan the biggest, most flashy expensive wedding you've ever seen. I got a bonus for this case."

"Don't treat me like a hysterical woman, Sean. I'm not eighteen years old. You can't bribe me with a fancy wedding—and I'm not desperate."

He gazed down at Allie with a patronizing look. "A few weeks ago, you were desperate to get me into bed."

"On our honeymoon," she emphasized. "Let's say I've come to my senses. You do realize, Sean, that you have given me *no* explanation for what you've been doing the past month. Nor have you given me *any* kind of real apology. You couldn't take five minutes to call me on what was supposed to be our wedding night and let me know you weren't dead or in jail? Even now, you can't even get down on one knee and beg me to marry you. You merely try to seduce me—as if this past month never happened."

"Baby, honey—"

"You're pathetic, Sean. I've never been so hurt in my life. You haven't even asked how I'm doing. You're not even curious about what I'm doing here in this house. You haven't asked about my apartment, if I still have my job, my family, let alone my sanity."

He gave her a grin. "You seem pretty sane to me. And pretty hot—"

Allie tried not to punch him in the face. "How do I know you won't do this to me again? How can I ever trust you? You threw me off for a case that any other lawyer in your office could have taken over—the other lawyers who were supposed to take over while you were gone on your honeymoon."

"But that case honed my sleuthing skills. I used them to find you here in podunk Heartland Cove County."

Allie stared at him in disbelief—and then she began to laugh. "Wouldn't my hometown be the first place you'd look? My parents were at the wedding, including my sister, my brother, my best friend, the minister and one hundred guests. Don't forget the wedding cake, a stack of gifts *and* Courtney Willis from the office, smiling at my misfortune behind her hand. Have you seen *her* lately, Sean, huh?"

"Well, yeah, of course. She's at the office every day. She's my secretary now and she helped me find my client that day."

"Isn't that convenient!" Allie felt her eyes fill with tears when she thought of watching Courtney Willis leave the church that afternoon, only to hook up with Sean and go searching together. *They* had managed to be in communication with each other.

Sean gave Allie a disappointed look. "Sarcasm has never become you, sweetheart."

She prickled at his term of endearment. "You haven't seen true sarcasm yet, buddy. What else did you do on our wedding night? Enjoy a celebratory dinner with Courtney, your partner in crime?"

"Stop it, Allie," Sean said, pulling her against him, his arms locked around her waist. She stood still as a statue, unmoving. "This is silly. We're meant to be together. We could get married today. You still have your wedding dress, right? Just call your family and have them meet us at the courthouse."

"It's Saturday," Allie told him. "The courthouse is closed." She wanted to yell at him some more, but the days of crying herself to sleep had drained her. It would be so easy to give in to Sean, the man she'd loved for so long. At the same time, she wanted to tell him to jump off the Heartland Cove Bridge and swim back to Toronto.

"I've missed you, Allie," he said, placing his hands against her cheeks. He turned her head towards him, sensing the fight going out of her. A moment later, his lips were on hers again, his tongue teasing against her mouth. "Come away with me. You know you want to."

Allie's throat swelled with frustration. That was part of the problem. Sean made her feel weak. As if he only had to snap his fingers and she'd follow him like a good puppy dog.

Behind them, the front door suddenly opened, banging against the wall.

Ethan's figure loomed large, his voice louder than Allie had ever heard before, words crisp with indignation. "Who the hell are you? Take your hands off Allie!"

Sean's eyes did a slow appraisal of Ethan Smith. "Since when does the help barge into his employer's house?"

Ethan didn't miss a beat. "When 'the help' owns the house," he retorted evenly.

"Oh, hey, sorry buddy," Sean said, completely oblivious.

Allie extricated herself from underneath Sean's arm, and walked toward Ethan, but stopped halfway between the two men.

"Ethan, this is Sean Carter. Sean, this is Ethan Smith—and yes, Ethan owns this house. I'm renting it."

Sean narrowed his eyes. "I still find it funny that he just walked in without knocking. Even bad landlords don't walk all over a person's privacy. I can sue him for you if you'd like."

"You're not suing anybody! Stop being a lawyer for two minutes, okay? And, um," Allie stammered. "He's here – because—"

She could feel Ethan bristle. He'd assessed the scene quite accurately, and he wasn't going to back off. "What she's trying to say is that I live here, too. But I was just packing to leave."

Sean gripped Allie's arm. "You just exploded on me with all

this righteous indignation about leaving you at the altar—meanwhile you're shacking up with some stranger?"

"I'm not shacking up with anyone!" Allie snapped. She'd had enough of both of them. "There was a rental misunderstanding—oh, why do I bother to try to explain—my bedroom is upstairs, Ethan's downstairs. And for your information, Sean, Ethan living in his own house as a temporary roommate isn't even in the same league as you disappearing for a month without a single word. You essentially broke up with me so you have no claim on me. None."

"Sweetheart," Sean began, moving toward her.

Allie stepped back against the fireplace hearth. "Don't touch me."

Sean threw a fierce look at Ethan. "Get your stuff and leave, buddy. Can't you see that Allie and I are trying to work things out?"

"Is that what you call this? A reconciliation?" Sarcasm overlaid Ethan's voice. "I'd say you're harassing Allie."

The testosterone in the room was making Allie ill. "This isn't a reconciliation and Sean isn't harassing me, but I want you both to leave. Now. If I want to speak with either one of you, I'll call you. Don't call me."

She went to the front door and opened it, staring daggers at them both and making it obvious that they both needed to leave immediately.

The two men were having a stare-down of their own. Finally, Ethan reached down to grab a box sitting behind one of the sofas. Without a backward glance, he charged through the front door and hauled it to his car. Not thirty seconds later, the man peeled out of the driveway and was down the street.

Allie's chest tightened. She hated for Ethan to leave on such poor terms, but she found herself feeling a bit annoyed with him as well.

"Next?" she said pointedly to Sean, keeping her distance.

"I can stay, Allie," Sean told her. "I'm sure you need a shoulder to cry on. I'm here for you. I took three days off from work."

"Three whole days? Wow, Sean, you really thought you could win me back in seventy-two hours? That's audacity at a level ten."

"We'll talk. We'll go to dinner. We'll work this out, sweetheart. You'll see. This bad month will soon be forgotten."

Allie threw up her hands. "You don't get it, Sean. Even after everything I've said the past hour you don't get it one iota. Leave, please. I'm about to pass out from a massive headache."

"I'll make that herbal tea you like so much and we can snuggle on the couch like old times."

He spoke as if they did that every evening—not! Maybe the man was delusional. His memories of their past were very different from her memories.

"No! Go, Sean, before I take a baseball bat to you."

Bending over, Sean picked up his suitcase and briefcase, both monogrammed with his initials. Allie almost laughed, recognizing the briefcase as the one he took with him to the office. Three days off? Right! The man had brought work with him.

"I'll be at the bed & breakfast when you need me. And you have my cell number, of course."

Allie bit her lips. A lot of good his cell phone had done her on their wedding day.

He leaned in for a kiss as he brushed past her on the way to the door. She stepped backward, out of reach. "Goodnight, Sean."

He paused on the threshold. "Take a shower and put on a pretty dress, Allie. We could have a night on the town."

"This town—ha! And no." Inwardly, Allie rolled her eyes. Seeing Sean—a stranger in town—would have everyone gossiping, the last thing she wanted to encourage from nosy neighbors.

She could just picture people staring, taking pictures, curious. Dear Lord in heaven, *no.*

Sean had stayed strictly with her life in Toronto. To have him here in her hometown almost felt wrong. He didn't belong here.

Sean's breath brushed across her face and she suddenly realized that she smelled mint gum. To cover up the shot of whiskey he must have had earlier. Of course, he would find the only bar in town before he showed up on her doorstep. The nerve he had, the gall to assume she'd run into his arms the moment he showed up.

Did the man presume those things because she had behaved exactly that way for the past five years? It was a sobering revelation to learn about herself.

Sean let go of the doorjamb, giving her a mournful gaze as he reluctantly dropped down the porch steps to the driveway. He'd actually had the nerve to think he could seduce her.

A sharp pain sliced at Allie's temples. Ibuprofen—pronto.

She closed the door hard, and then immediately locked it.

CHAPTER 16

By midnight, Allie had received three calls from Sean, none of which she answered. She finally turned off the sound and then turned off the television that sat on the bureau of the master suite, shows she'd been watching dully, without a single coherent thought in her mind.

After a long hot bath, Allie shut off the lights and burrowed into her pillow, the window cracked for fresh air.

Allie's mind spun with the events of the day. It had been such a shock to see Sean at her door.

He *had* made the effort to come a thousand kilometers to Heartland to see her, leaving behind his work and important cases—not something he'd ever done before. Not since his father had passed away three years earlier. At that time, Sean had been gone exactly four days. Two for travel, one for the funeral and the fourth to help his mother go through financial paperwork.

He was giving her three days—and nobody had died. Maybe it meant something, maybe it didn't. But his secretary was still Courtney Mills, his previous girlfriend.

Sean *knew* how much Allie despised the gloating woman. The woman who had broken up with Sean for another man—a pro baseball player who lavished Courtney with gifts and took her to the best parties and spent vacations on first class cruises and five star hotels.

Once upon a time this had made Allie feel sorry for Sean. He knew what it was to suffer, but that didn't seem to stop him from being obtuse about his own actions.

To show up after a month was ridiculous. Allie had spent these past weeks coming to terms with his actions, his obvious desire not to marry her, the embarrassment she'd suffered.

Except she knew that Sean didn't see it that way. He probably hadn't tried to purposely shame her. He just didn't think the same way. For him, it *was* easier to just reschedule and get on with his busy life.

Except, if a man truly loved a woman he wouldn't do that to her. Right?

"Right," Allie murmured into her pillow. She punched the downy filling and glanced at the clock. One thirty a.m. Darn it, why couldn't she sleep?

Rising groggily from the bed, she headed downstairs to get a glass of water and a sleeping pill.

Her phone blinked with text messages.

Not wanting to stir up her mind with more pleadings from Sean, Allie turned away, but after swallowing the sleeping tablet and crawling back under the covers, she reached for the cell phone, curiosity getting the better of her.

The messages weren't from Sean. They were from Ethan.

10:38 p.m. My grandmother was delighted to meet you. Asked if I'd bring you back sometime.

10:53 p.m. She was quite taken with you . . . as I am . . . but no pressure.

11:17 p.m. Allie. I'll wait. I'm good at waiting. I'm here if you ever need someone to talk to, or a shoulder to cry on.

11:20 p.m. I have pretty empathetic shoulders like that.

Allie snorted at the funny, innocent way he had. She didn't

want to give in to his humor, but Ethan did make her laugh. She never felt any pressure from him. Despite the secrecy of his photography and his future billions, he had never outright lied to her for a devious purpose. He was fairly steady and unassuming, such a different personality from Sean who was loud and brash and steamrolled over her.

There was a time that Allie had liked that about Sean. She saw it as confidence, a man driven by intelligence and ambition.

A man like Sean didn't usually make for a family-oriented husband and father though. She'd probably only see him late at night and on Sundays. He'd already worked his Saturdays for two years.

Allie rolled over, replaying the physical moments with Sean today. At first, her stomach had jumped when he kissed her, as it always had done in the past.

But now Sean's kisses made her want to pull away. He came on too strong. Too brusque. There was little tenderness, and she'd needed his tenderness, his thoughtfulness—especially after what he'd done to her.

But there had been none. His good looks and personality and high-powered presence didn't do it for her any longer.

Allie stared at the ceiling. What a strange revelation. For five years she thought she'd wanted one thing only, and now she was rejecting it.

Drifting off to sleep, Allie found her mind returning to that morning when Ethan had kissed her on the beach at Hopewell Rocks. His lips had been so warm, so soft, it startled her. She'd melted against his gentle sensitivity as she'd never done with Sean.

She could still feel the protective touch of his arms around her, shielding her from the world that had hurt her so much. And yet, there had also been a surprising dose of passion and romance, an overwhelming sexiness in the way his lips tasted hers.

Definitely, there had been an undercurrent of desire, but Ethan had kept himself in check with gentlemanly tenderness. He would never presume or pressure her.

Allie opened her eyes, staring through the lace curtains at the half moon shining through. She got the feeling Ethan would be one of those men that waited for intimacy until their wedding night. He'd give her that respect and deference. It was a startling revelation.

"What does it all mean?" she moaned. She'd never pictured herself with anybody but Sean Carter, and now she couldn't picture herself with him. Everything had turned upside-down.

The only thing to do was to tell both Sean and Ethan to leave town for a while. Or to stay out of her way. She needed time and space and no men in sight.

Of course, avoiding someone in a town the size of Heartland Cove was easier said than done.

Yawning, Allie placed her phone back on the night table. The red light flickered with another text message. This time from Sean.

1:47 a.m. I'm lonely without you, Allie.

1:53 a.m. You've hurt me so much. I can't believe you were living with a total stranger and not me.

1:58 a.m. I think we need couples counseling.

1:59 a.m. We can work through this.

Allie slammed the phone down. "Just shut up, Sean!"

Even after deserting her, he was still trying to control her. The arrogance. The superiority. The condescension.

"Get yourself some counseling, Sean Carter. Learn how to be a nice human being first."

When the cell phone rang, it was after two o'clock in the morning. Of course, it was Sean again. Ethan would never annoy her and then wake her up in the middle of the night.

Allie punched the phone off.

The next day she slept until ten.

THE NEIGHBOR'S SECRET

There were three more missed phone calls from Sean. One to say good morning. One to invite her to breakfast. And the last to ask her to marry him and check into the Heartland Cove Bed & Breakfast with him tonight.

As if all it took was a proposal without apology or explanation or groveling. Not that he needed to grovel, but Sean Carter needed to admit what he'd done. He needed to truly understand why she was so angry, and to empathize with *her,* and not his own hurt ego because she'd rejected him yesterday.

Was the man even in love with her?

Would you leave someone at the altar that you honestly, wholeheartedly loved?

Her gut feeling on that score was not encouraging.

Strangely, at the same time, she was feeling despondent that there wasn't a single call from Ethan. Maybe she'd scared him off. Maybe she'd been too irrational. What man would return after that?

While she got dressed, Allie started wondering if Ethan had slept in his car, especially if Sean had taken the only available room at the B&B.

At least the temperatures were warm. She should have thrown him a blanket and pillow because when Allie stood at the doorway to his bedroom, she noticed that the man had taken nothing with him, save his personal clothing and shaving gear.

Perhaps he'd driven into Somerville to find a room, or gone to his grandmother's house.

Allie put a hand to her chest as she made her way into the kitchen to fix a pot of tea. Ethan had told her he was falling for her—and had kissed her in the most utterly romantic way she'd ever been kissed.

"Oh, golly, I want Ethan to kiss me again like that," she told the tea kettle. "But it feels illegal."

While Allie ate a piece of cold, hard toast—goodness, she

missed Ethan's gourmet cooking—she made a quick call to her parents.

"Sorry I missed the ten o'clock tour bus, Dad!" she told him.

"Take the day off," he said promptly. "We have Erin here, and she's not too feisty on this sleepy Sunday."

"You're awesome, Dad, thank you."

"I heard some news from a little bird, sweetheart."

Allie's heart began to thump. "Oh? What was that?"

"You know this town is too small to keep secrets, but if you want to keep it your business, I won't pry, honey."

"Dad, you're too good—and probably not nosey enough. Yes, Sean Carter showed up yesterday. Yes, I talked to him. No, he isn't here at the house. And I'm not sure I'm seeing him again. We sort of argued."

She could picture her father nodding to himself, observant and intuitive, despite his quiet ways. "I can understand that. Your mother and I are with you on whatever you decide."

"Thanks, Dad. Honestly, I have no idea what I'm going to do."

"I have faith in you, sweetheart. You'll figure it out. Now I need to get that last teenager of mine to start picking up trash before the next bus."

"Keeping up the town's appearances should be embedded into our DNA," Allie said with a laugh.

As soon as her father hung up, the cell phone rang again.

Allie let out a groan and almost ignored it, but quickly snatched it up when she saw that it was Marla.

"Hey, girl, I've got some pictures to develop and mount, want to help me? I promised the client I'd have them done by Monday."

"Eek, Marla, that's tomorrow."

"Yeah, that's why I'm calling you. It's officially time to hang up the shingle for *Marla's Magical Moments*."

"So you're sticking with the sappy business name?" Allie teased.

"Hey, we live in a sappy town so it fits." Marla paused. "Can I set up at your place? I have absolutely no room here at my folks and I think you rented the last place in town. Housing is hard to come by, you know."

"Sure," Allie said slowly. The only place would be Ethan's room and the adjoining room, known as the morning room a hundred years ago.

Which meant he'd never return. He was gone. Allie rubbed at her neck, emotion pricking behind her eyes. Maybe she was just tired, but the idea of never seeing Ethan again wasn't something that gave her any pleasure.

"I'm probably being melodramatic," she said aloud. "He's still working to stop the mayor and he's renovating some property for the historical society. I'll see him sometime around town."

But Allie had a feeling Ethan would stay under the radar. Besides, she wouldn't live in Heartland Cove forever. She needed to go back to her job at the bank in a few weeks. Her boss was very generous and checked in with her once a week, but she didn't plan on slinging fries for the rest of her life. She had her business degree, after all.

"Time to move on, Allie Strickland," she voiced aloud, sticking her plate and tea cup into the mostly empty dishwasher. Deep in her gut, she knew she didn't really want to return to Toronto for any other reason than to retrieve her belongings out of storage.

But that meant moving somewhere else and starting over. The thought of hunting for a job with its accompanying resumes and interviews was incredibly depressing.

After sticking her hair into a ponytail, she was ready for Marla when her friend arrived.

"Okay, girl, spill it all," were the first words out of Marla's mouth. "I just about screamed when I saw Sean Carter having dinner at the lobster house last night."

"Um, hi," Allie said, tugging Marla into the morning room. "Yeah, I guess a lot happened yesterday."

While Allie related the events of the day before, they spread out Marla's photo developing gear as well as hung up black-out curtains while Allie told her about her brunch date with Ethan's grandmother and then their fight. And *then* Sean showing up and the subsequent fight with him.

"Whoa, girl, what a day!"

"I tell you, I'm all fought out."

Marla finished tacking up the end of a black curtain over the yellowing Victorian lace ones and stared at Allie. "You mean you're taking him back?"

"Of course not. He needs to grovel first."

Marla arched an eyebrow really high. "You think Sean Carter is actually going to get on his knees and beg for you to come back to him?"

"Wouldn't you hold out for a really good apology? I mean, he put me through a horror show."

"I know, sweetie, I know." Marla put an arm around Allie. "I've never seen you so distraught. Anybody would be. He ruined your wedding day."

"No, it was more than just a wedding. He ruined my life. Tore my trust and belief in love and honesty to shreds." Allie paused. "What would you have done?"

"I wouldn't have married Sean Carter in the first place."

"What!" Allie yelped. "You never told me that."

A guilty look came over Marla. "I knew you were in love with him. How could I tell you not to when you'd been together for so many years? But I was worried that he wouldn't make you happy."

Allie was aghast. "Did you suspect he'd actually stand me up on our wedding day?"

Marla shook her head. "No, but I wasn't shocked either. His career is super, super important to him."

"That's the understatement of the year. He tried to stay here last night. He called me over and over again after I kicked him out. The worst part? He never apologized or explained." Allie chewed on her lip. "Now I wonder if I ever gave him a chance to, I was so mad . . ." her voice trailed off.

Marla let out a snort. "A rip-roaring apology should have been the first words out of his mouth!"

"He did say he missed me."

"Do *not* defend him. He only missed your body."

Allie slumped at the table, tracing her fingers along the carved and painted wooden sign. Marla's brother had done a superb job. It was creative and professional.

"I need to pound some nails," she finally said. "Let's go put this up. We'll hang it from the mailbox out at the road. I think there are a few tools in the garage."

A few minutes later, armed with a box of nails and an old hammer, they headed down the driveway. Marla had come equipped with her own posts and rings. They took turns pounding the posts into the dirt and then hung the sign so that it swung in the light breeze.

"It looks fantastic," Allie said, admiring their work.

Marla clapped her hands. "Perfect. Now I'll get those business cards ordered. Shall we get some lunch before we dive into developing fluid?"

"I have lunch stuff here. I really don't want to leave the house today. I'm afraid of running into Sean or Ethan."

Marla gave her a devious smile. "What else did you do with Ethan Smith yesterday before you met dear old granny?"

"What gave you the impression we did anything else?" Allie turned away to dig into the refrigerator for the deli meat and cheese. She was afraid that her thoughts were strewn across her face.

"You don't go visit someone's *grandmother* without it meaning something."

"She's lonely," Allie said vaguely. "I agreed to go along to meet her. She's really something though, lovely and smart as a whip. I think Ethan wanted to prove that his photography was completely above board. His grandmother is the president of the Heartland Cove County Historical Society. He's doing some work for her." Not *exactly* true, but close enough.

"Did you go anywhere else? To his excavation site?"

Allie opened the cupboards to search for a bag of Covered Bridge Potato Chips. She knew Ethan had purchased some the previous week, and she had a craving for the best potato chips in the world.

"I always know when you're hiding something."

Allie widened her eyes, but it didn't work.

"Okay, keep it coming, girl," Marla demanded.

"We had some time to kill and stopped at Hopewell Rocks for a short walk. Gosh, it's been years since I went there. It's always too cold to go when I visit in the winter for my Christmas break."

"The beach is always a romantic setting." Marla's eyes were all-knowing, and she was grinning. "Was the tide in or out?"

"Out." One word answers were probably best.

"Did he hold your hand while you walked?"

"No." Allie glanced away as she replayed in her mind how gentlemanly Ethan took her hand and slipped it through his arm to make sure she didn't slip down the algae-covered slick rocks or accidentally step into an unseen tide pool. "Not exactly," she added, as though she couldn't stop herself from saying the words—and immediately kicked herself. Why couldn't she keep her mouth shut?

"I knew it!" Marla said triumphantly. "I suspected there was some sort of spark going on between you two. You would never have let another man live downstairs."

"I had no choice! The rental agreement—the misunderstanding."

"You know, *my* grandmother used to say *poppycock*. Women always have choices. Okay, go on."

"Marla, stop it. It was a lovely morning, actually. Maybe that's why I was doubly shocked at Sean showing up out of nowhere. I hadn't thought about him all that day."

"You're turning this back around to Sean. Tell me about Ethan."

Allie grew exasperated. "He made sure I didn't slip as we walked. Are you satisfied?"

"A male buddy doesn't usually do that. They race you to the bottom of the stairs, or give you a headlock, or some other manly act. Not grand gestures. No manners."

"Ethan is very well-mannered." A small smile crept across her lips, which she immediately cursed when Marla pounced again.

"Just tell me one thing, Miss Secretive. Is he a good kisser?"

"Marla!"

Allie jammed the last piece of ham onto the sandwiches, slapped mustard onto the bread slices, crammed them together on a paper plate and handed it over. No china for her.

"Eat your lunch," she ordered.

"I love the look of guilt on your face," Marla said. "Ethan Smith must be a most excellent kisser."

Allie plopped into her chair and wanted to cry. She'd driven Ethan away, but she was so darn confused by him, and by Sean.

Maybe she needed to run away again, only this time to New York City and lose herself in the crowds. Forget about Sean once and for all. Forget Ethan and his childhood crush and his sweet grandmother and his chef skills and his smile and his deep brown eyes. And those lips.

"Yes, Marla," she said, staring down at her uneaten sandwich. "Ethan Smith kissed me. Kissed me like nobody else ever has."

And that was before she learned that he was an obnoxiously wealthy man.

She didn't tell Marla about Ethan's inheritance and old money as one of Heartland Cove's founders. That bit of gossip wasn't hers to broadcast. Perhaps Miss Ellie would change her will and give it to charity, or some other long-lost cousin.

The money didn't make a bit of difference. Even if there wasn't a fat 401K, Allie had to keep reminding herself that he was on track to inherit half of Heartland Cove. It might not be liquidated money, but it was there, and it belonged to Benjamin Ethan Miles AKA Ethan Smith.

Marla's gaze was unflinching. "I haven't seen you two together on your own, only that day walking down the road, but now that I think about it, you *have* been smiling a lot lately—except when you're cussing out the ex-fiancé."

Allie gulped. "Problem is, I may never see Ethan again. I threw him out, too."

"Oh, Allie," Marla said with a soft laugh. "You're impossible when you're in love."

CHAPTER 17

"Bite your tongue," Allie said flippantly, snapping open a Diet Coke to get a shot of caffeine

She missed Ethan, but to say she was in love with him was preposterous. She'd only known him a month. His kisses were an impetuous move, inspired by a romantic beach. It meant nothing.

"So tell me more about this mysterious Ethan Smith," Marla said. "There have never been any Smiths in Heartland Cove."

"You're right," Allie said with an elusive air.

"I hear he's a local."

"Where did you hear that?"

"Oh, I don't know," Marla said airily and just as vaguely. "The bartender at Sal's place?"

Allie narrowed her eyes. "What's Ethan's reputation?"

"No, you tell me, my nebulous, hazy, imprecise friend."

"You don't have to call names," Allie said, laughing. "I give up. His grandmother is Elizabeth Stewart. Go look up their genealogy."

"Such a smarty-pants, Allie Strickland. Just watch me. I will.

I'd head to the library right now if we didn't have photo mounting to do this afternoon."

The photos were dry by early afternoon, the negatives hanging like laundry on the line in the blacked-out bedroom.

Being in the guest room that Ethan had slept in brought thoughts of him to the surface. What did he think of her after the fight with Sean? Did he think she'd been lying to him? Had she ruined her life on every possible level?

She and Ethan had both fibbed about their identities and past lives before they were so rudely thrown together by a scatter-brained Viola Stark.

The photo chemicals soon stunk up the entire house with their peculiar sharp odor. Allie opened windows and shut the doors to the rooms upstairs as well as the kitchen and morning room.

The two of them spent the afternoon bumping into each other in the darkroom, Allie taking orders from Marla.

"Marla's Magical Moments has some seriously good cameras—and a good eye," she said with a grin. "These are gorgeous."

A few of the photos were experimental, taken around town, including pictures of the tourists in line at the vendors along the Saint John's. "These candid shots are really good. Humanity at its most humorous and poignant."

"I was trying out various lenses and settings. To see what my new camera could do."

"Was the camera expensive?"

Marla snorted. "It will take ten weddings to pay it off."

"Seriously?"

"Only by half, but it's a camera I'll have for years and I'm already seeing improvement in myself. I'm so excited about the wedding I've got booked for next Saturday. Will you come help me carry equipment and fluff the bride's wedding train?"

"I can fluff wedding dresses with the best of them." But Allie's smile was tight. It would be the first wedding since her own canceled one. "Seeing the happy bride and groom may cause me to fall over keening with howls, though. Just warning you."

"I'm sorry, Allie. I wasn't thinking. Of course you don't have to come. What an idiot I am."

"Hey, if we're going to run *Marla's Magical Moments* together I'd better get back on the horse, right?"

"You mean you're getting married again?"

Allie burst out laughing. "That's not what I meant."

"Free champagne is always fun, but we have to stay sober until the end."

"The job has perks besides working with my best friend?"

Marla gave her a quick hug. "Next up is discussing our long-term goals."

Allie's business degree kicked in. "Marketing, advertising, publicity, costs, prices, supplies."

"Whew, slow down!"

"You take the pictures and I'll worry about the rest."

"Weddings every weekend if I can book them, so get ready to throw your social life out the window."

"I don't have a social life now," Allie said, making a face.

Marla packed up her camera, checked the bag for lenses and paraphernalia, and the two of them headed down to the bridge.

"I'm going to check out good spots for snagging unwary tourists," Marla said, rubbing her hands together in glee while Allie parked the car behind the family fry truck.

Not two minutes later, Mrs. Strickland came running out the back door. "You must have read my mind, Allie. Erin took off in the pickup to buy more potatoes out at the Hillside Potato Farm. The buses have been packed and another will be here in fifteen minutes. I know it's your day off, but can you—"

"Hey, I'm perfectly fine to take pictures while you help out, Allie," Marla told her. "Someone watching will just make me nervous."

"A lame excuse. You don't know what the word nervous means."

With a wink and a wave, Marla went off to find tourists to offer them the seasonal *Marla's Magical Moments* discount.

After putting on a clean apron, Allie went into gear, peeling and slicing and frying and seasoning.

When Erin showed up, her mother ran to the rear of the long, narrow truck to help unload the potatoes and Allie manned the front window to ring up sales while her father kept cooking.

The line was longer than normal at the height of summer.

When she looked up after the tenth customer, Sean Carter reached out a hand and stopped her pencil moving across the sales pad.

"Allie," he said.

Her heart went into a stutter. "Sean! What are you doing here?"

"You won't answer my phone calls or texts."

"Did it ever occur to you that I might have some really good reasons?" Allie snapped, and then cringed, aware of the tourists standing right behind him. "This is your second day in Heartland and you have yet to apologize for not showing up at our wedding. You want to pick up as if nothing happened. I call that being a jerk, Sean. Honestly."

The woman behind him in line stared at Allie and then nodded, glancing up at her husband and giving him an elbow in the side.

"Honestly, you need to give me a chance—"

"You had so many chances and you deny it. It's like you blame *me*."

"That day was insanely crazy, sweetheart."

"Do you hear yourself? Your *day* was crazy? I had the worst day of my *life*. Our wedding was about our *lives* together. It wasn't just an event or another work day, or overtime."

Allie's voice rose with every sentence. She tried to calm down,

THE NEIGHBOR'S SECRET

but for some reason she couldn't, despite the stares—and glares—she was receiving from gawking tourists. Even people sitting in chairs around the area enjoying the beautiful weather had begun to glance around, sensing tension in the air.

"I can make this right, sweetheart," Sean said in a low voice.

"Stop calling me sweetheart!"

"I can't help it. You're the woman I'm meant to be with, even if it takes a few more weeks to plan the wedding again."

"Listen to yourself, Sean!" Allie snapped.

"Can we go somewhere else to talk?" Sean finally said, his face turning red when he realized how much they were being overheard.

"No. You can speak to me right here in front of my family and my town. You shouldn't have anything to hide. You need to be straight up honest with me."

Allie felt a tiny bit of guilt forcing him to address his actions right there in public even though he hated confrontation, but she wasn't backing down.

Sean heaved a sigh of irritation. "I came all this way and you won't talk to me in private. I have to get back to the city. The judge has moved up my court day to tomorrow instead of Wednesday so I'm going to have to drive all night. I'll be beat."

Allie dropped her pencil in astonishment. "You'll be beat. Poor baby," she said sarcastically. "If you were serious about winning me back you'd stay and make this right. You would be here to woo me, to court me, and to do everything you could to make me fall in love with you all over again. And you haven't made a single attempt. It's like you're incapable of having any empathy or understanding."

The woman in line began to slowly clap her hands. Her husband blushed and put an arm around her.

A wave of sudden emotion filled Allie's throat, and she knew exactly what she had to do. "Sean, it's over. Your behavior the past two days has convinced me. You need to go home."

"When will you return to Toronto?"

"I'm not sure I'll ever go back."

"Will you let me know?"

Allie shook her head. "Probably not."

He arched an eyebrow. "I'm not convinced you mean it, but I have to get back. My career is on the line. It's one of my most important cases."

"It's always about *your* career, Sean." Allie slammed the register door closed and it popped back open. She slammed it again. With every slam she grew more livid. If only she could be fifteen again and throw a bag of greasy fries at him—or pour an ice cold Coke over his head. It would ruin his suit, but the sight would give her immense satisfaction.

She picked up a cup and hit the button to fill it with ice water. Her father suddenly spoke over her shoulder. "Let me take over here, Allie. Go on to the back and tell Sean goodbye."

"Thank you, Mr. Strickland," Sean said.

Allie spun on her heel and stalked to the back of the shop. When she threw open the back door, Sean was already there. He tugged at her arm. "Come outside with me."

"No," Allie refused, stubbornness rising like a growing tidal wave.

"You're being unreasonable," Sean told her with a woeful look. "I don't want to leave like this. I'll call you when I get back."

"Don't bother."

He let out a huge sigh. "Okay, will it make you feel better if I admit that maybe I don't have it in me to get married right now?"

Allie folded her arms and leaned back against a stack of shelves, letting out a gasp of surprise. "Now you admit it? You could have said something months ago."

"Maybe our timing was wrong. Maybe I can get serious about marriage and a family when I'm more established and not trying to please the boss."

THE NEIGHBOR'S SECRET

"Maybe your boss is the only one you want to please," she said, her voice hard.

"Come on, don't do this. I want to leave on good terms."

"I don't think that's possible, Sean."

"Give me an inch, Allie, please," he pleaded. "Can we be friends? Can I have one last kiss goodbye? You know I'm going to miss you."

Tears smarted now and Allie's eyes grew blurry. Pulling away, she reached for the box of tissues on the shelf perched above the deep fat fryer, currently sizzling with frying potatoes.

All at once, Sean barreled inside the fry truck. He tugged at her arm, whirling her around and pulling her waist into his.

His lips came down on hers, as if he owned her. How dare he force himself on her? As if a kiss was all it took for her to give in and agree to everything he wanted.

She tried to speak and their teeth knocked together so hard it hurt. His arms gripped hers like a vise. "Stop it, Sean. You took away every shred of my dreams, and you still want a piece of me. I almost can't stand to look at you. Please go now. Go!"

But he wouldn't release her. Allie wiggled her arms out of his and tried to push him away, but she was knocked off balance in the process and her hip slammed into the edge of the deep fat fryer.

The fryer tipped over and boiling oil splattered across her torso, scorching her arms and hands. "Dear God!" she screamed.

Horror seeped up her throat as she watched the hot oil melt her apron, coiling the material into horrific patterns of black.

Before she could move, the cascading oil spilled onto the gas flames underneath the fryer, and plumes of fire shot up toward the ceiling.

Allie's screams rent the air as her parents and sister ran to douse the fire but more flames shot in every direction. In seconds, the walls of the fry shop were leaping with flames, licking at the ceiling in raging orange and red.

119

"Fire! Fire!" someone yelled.

More voices called for the fire department while heat seared Allie. Time seemed to slow. It was like watching a horror movie with herself in the middle of it, her clothes and hair smoking.

Dad's voice yelled, a thunder above the clamor. "Allie, drop and roll. Drop and roll!"

Mom ran for the fire extinguisher and that's when Allie realized that Erin was nowhere to be seen.

"Where's Erin?" she screamed, her throat raw. The front of the shop was filled with flames, taking down the cupboards and counters in seconds.

Black smoke rolled through the shop in ugly ripples. *So* fast. So instantly, Allie didn't have time to think.

Allie had turned into a column of heat, just like Lot's wife had turned into a pillar of salt. She wanted to obey her father's voice, but she was in such pain she couldn't get her legs to move, let alone bend to drop to the floor.

An instant later, a tall male came out of nowhere and picked her up in his arms, slapping at her torso and arms and legs to stop the sparks from spreading, running with her out of the tiny shop and laying her on the lawn by the river.

She screamed in pain, her eyes burning with such pain from the acrid smoke she couldn't see who it was.

The sun's rays were on her face while a nasty burnt smell encompassed the entire world. A moment later she began to cough, hacking as if she'd just smoked an entire carton of Marlboro's in five minutes flat.

"Allie, Allie!" The same person who had dragged her outside was trying to get her to speak, but she couldn't seem to move her mouth to form words. The world was a haze of smoke and torture.

"Dad," she finally croaked.

"It's Ethan," he whispered, squeezing her hand.

"Dad. Mom." Oh, it hurt to talk.

THE NEIGHBOR'S SECRET

"Your father is fine. So are your mother and sister."

Her family was there. They were okay. The relief was so enormous tears dripped from Allie's eyes.

Somewhere behind her, she heard a horrible, rending crash as though the world was falling apart. Cringing, Allie instinctively ducked her head.

"Ssh, ssh, it's okay, Allie," Ethan said. "I've got you. You're going to be okay. But I'm afraid the roof of the fry shack just collapsed."

Her mother's voice was suddenly there and Allie managed to crack open one eyelid. Her parents and Erin surrounded her. And that's when Allie began to cry, but the tears burned her cheeks as if hot acid was pouring from her tear ducts.

"Hold my hand, Allie," Ethan told her firmly. "Don't faint. Don't pass out. Keep hanging onto me. An ambulance is coming."

"It hurts, it hurts," she whimpered, unable to stop herself. She bit down on her lip and tasted blood. Then the wail of a siren came to her ears.

When her eyelids fluttered, Ethan's face came into view, blurry and unfocused, but she could see that his eyes were fixed on hers. Intense and deeply worried.

"I can see you," she whispered. She closed them again because the sunlight hurt.

"Good girl," Ethan said hoarsely. " You're in shock, but you're going to be fine."

His lips brushed against her hair and Allie sensed rather than saw the emotion he was holding back.

Once the ambulance arrived and the paramedics lifted her onto the gurney, she screamed in a burst of fresh agony when they slid her inside and slammed the doors.

Vaguely, Allie was aware that her full-length apron had charred to a crisp. Her jeans had black holes burned down to the skin of her thighs. She couldn't remember what color her blouse had been, but only part of it was left. Even the lace on her bra had melted.

Dirt crunched along her teeth, but someone behind her said that she was just tasting ash in her mouth. A moment later, there was a prick in her arm as the paramedics got an IV going. It wasn't long before Allie melted into the narrow stretcher and disappeared into oblivion.

CHAPTER 18

Allie woke to a low-lit hospital room at the Upper River Valley Hospital in Waterville. She gazed down at herself. Clean white sheets. One of those blue checked hospital gowns she saw on daytime soap opera television. She tested her fingers and toes, bending her knees slightly.

She could move. Her left hand hurt, and her right leg hurt—a lot—but otherwise she seemed fine. Not too much pain anywhere else at the moment. Just groggy as heck.

Marla's face came into view. "Hey, sleepy head. How do you feel?"

Allie blinked slowly. "Um, okay, I guess?"

"You scared the heck out of us—the whole town, actually."

"What time is it?"

"Tuesday morning. And breakfast just arrived."

Allie glanced at the hospital tray coming toward her, loaded with scrambled eggs, a biscuit, and a cup of fruit. She wasn't hungry. Maybe some hot tea with lemon for her raging sore throat. Was she coming down sick with strep?

"I slept all night?"

"A night and a day, but you were sedated in case you were in pain," Marla told her. "But everybody knows sleep isn't real in a hospital. The nurses just pretend it is."

"Where are my parents, and Erin?"

"They're at your folks' home. They were here until midnight until—well, the staff told them you were going to be perfectly fine and finally convinced them to go home. They'll be back to see you after you eat this hearty, well-balanced breakfast."

"I'm not hungry." Allie jiggled her head, trying to shake the images swimming around her head into some semblance of coherence. "What happened? It's all a fuzzy blur. The last thing I remember was Sean and me—arguing, as usual." Allie's voice croaked. Her mouth was so dry.

"Here, have a sip of water." A male nurse appeared at her other side and helped her sip from a straw. The drink finally began to clear her confusion.

Allie stared at him. The nurse wasn't a nurse at all. It was Ethan Smith holding the cup, his face bending over hers. Worry swallowed up his entire countenance.

"Ethan," Allie said hoarsely. "You were there. I remember now."

"Memory might not be a good thing," he said with a self-deprecating laugh.

"Why are you here so early in the morning?" Their own argument from a few days ago flooded back into her mind and Allie flushed at the memory of when she banished him from the house.

Marla jumped in to answer. "The man never left. He's been here all night keeping watch over you."

A sheepish expression crossed Ethan's face when he shrugged at her, his mouth curving up into a small smile.

Allie bit her lips, worry rising up her belly. "Tell me the truth. Am I scarred? Am I ugly—" her voice broke. She wanted a mirror to assess the damage, but if she was maimed Allie didn't know if she could handle seeing her reflection again.

Ethan snatched up her un-bandaged, unhurt hand. "Not a

THE NEIGHBOR'S SECRET

chance, Allie. You're the most beautiful woman I've ever known. No matter what happens to you, I'll never stop thinking that."

Allie couldn't let him get away with it. "Liar," she sputtered.

Ethan shook his head. "I don't lie."

Allie arched an eyebrow.

"Except when I'm trying to hide my bank account," he joked.

Laughter sputtered up her chest, and then Allie had a coughing fit. Ethan placed a hand on her shoulder, but Allie didn't want him feeling sorry for her.

"I don't get it," Marla complained. "What's the joke?"

Ethan gave her a mysterious smile. "A private one."

That just made Allie laugh again, but fear was growing in her chest. "Okay, give it to me straight, you guys. What's the damage? I'm on pain meds so I can't tell. My left hand is bandaged so I'm assuming it's burned."

Before Marla or Ethan could answer her, a doctor walked in wearing the usual white lab coat over hospital scrubs, and carrying a clipboard. Short white hair curled around her ears and a hospital badge dangled around her neck, but Allie couldn't read the small print.

"I'm Doctor Hancock and you are a lucky woman, Miss Strickland."

"That's what I was trying to tell her," Ethan said. His hand slipped slowly down Allie's arm, and when he touched the skin just above her wrist a shiver ran down her neck.

She could tell he wanted to hold her hand, but he was sitting on her left side where the white gauze made a definite barrier to any sort of skin contact.

"I'm a little numb on different parts of my body. Do I have bandages on my head or face that I can't see? Do I still have a nose, or a mouth?"

The doctor smiled. "Your face is perfectly fine, no burns. The only serious burns are on your left hand and right thigh. A spot on your stomach only needs Neosporin for a few days and shouldn't scar at all."

Allie swallowed hard, wondering if she'd ever be able to sit down and type at a keyboard or throw a ball, or play the piano. Not that she was a pianist, but she wanted to know she still had options.

"What's the treatment from here on out?" she asked.

"In two days, you'll come to my regular office and we'll change the bandages. Probably two or three times and then the bandages come off and some ointments and salves will do the rest of the work. Your skin will be tender for a few weeks, but after that, you're going to be like new again."

"Really? That's all?" Allie could still see the flames and hear the crashing of the roof in her mind. She shuddered with a sudden chill.

"You're a lucky girl, Allie," Doctor Hancock repeated with a smile. "Lucky that someone got you out of there so fast. The discharge papers are here. You can sign them or someone else can do that if you're not feeling up to it."

"Discharge?" Allie echoed. "You mean I'm leaving?"

"No reason to keep you here. The burns are second to a minus third degree level so you're good to go. Don't get the skin or bandages wet. Follow the release instructions. I'll see you in my office in forty-eight hours. The appointment time is on the paperwork."

Doctor Hancock gave a wave and strode out the door to her next patient.

There was a moment of silence and then Allie turned to Ethan. "I want to hit you. You're sitting there all—all emotional— and I'm fine. Or I will be, I guess."

He gazed into her face. "I *was* worried. All night. You looked really hurt when I helped put you into the ambulance. There's nothing left of the fry shop—it was sobering to watch all those volunteer fire fighters running with their gear and hoses down to the river—but it burned to the ground."

Allie let out a moan, thinking of her parents' livelihood gone. "I need to see Mom and Dad. Where are my regular clothes?" She tried to sit up, but her head spun. That was probably the pain killers, too.

"Slow down," Marla answered. "Your clothes went to the hospital incinerator. Charred right off your body."

Allie bit her lips, her eyes darting away from Ethan's face.

"Don't worry. I brought clothes from home." Marla held up a small suitcase. "Ethan let me inside the house."

Allie gulped in air. "I guess I never asked Ethan for the key when he left on Saturday."

"When you told me to leave," he reminded her. "And it is *my* key," he said, his mouth twitching in amusement.

Marla glanced between them. "Sometimes I think you two are talking in code."

"We won't get into past history." Allie shifted uncomfortably on the raised hospital bed. Quickly, she pulled the sheet up, realizing that she didn't have any underwear on.

Ethan's eyes crinkled. "We have plenty of time to argue again."

Allie signed the papers with a terrible scrawl and a nurse took them, returning a few minutes later to take her vitals. "We're not letting you go quite yet, young lady," the woman said.

"So . . . um, anybody seen Sean Carter around Heartland?" Allie tried to be nonchalant, but she was curious. The last time she'd seen him she'd pushed him away when he attacked her with that horrible kiss—just before the vat of hot oil tipped over.

Ethan glanced down and Marla licked her lips before unzipping the suitcase to check the contents.

"What aren't you two telling me?"

Marla hung a light summer dress on the hook of the bathroom door. "Do you want to tell her, or shall I?"

Ethan brushed his thick bangs out of his eyes. He rose from his chair. "Wow. Well."

"You're actually speechless?" Allie asked, giving him a smirk.

"Don't do that," he warned.

"Do what?" She gave him an innocent stare.

"That look. That smile." He shoved his hands into the pockets of his jeans. "You drive me crazy."

"He means in a good way," Marla interjected. "As in, he's head over heels for you."

Allie couldn't look at either one of them now. "Well, if nobody is going to tell me I'm going to get up and get dressed."

"That's my cue to leave," Ethan said, promptly walking out the door and closing it behind him.

"Is he coming back?" Allie asked, worried. "He didn't even say goodbye."

"He's not leaving; he's in the hall to give you privacy. And he's driving you home, silly! It's Tuesday afternoon and I have some crowds to shoot. Pictures, that is."

If it was Tuesday, that meant the meeting with the mayor and taken place the day before. Allie's head swam when she swung her legs over and put her toes on the cool linoleum.

"You need help up?"

"No, I'm okay. My throat hurts though."

"Before you woke up, the doctor mentioned that might happen. Smoke inhalation, but the chest x-ray showed no lingering effects or damage. But the doc said to use throat lozenges liberally. There are a couple on your tray over there."

Allie put her fists on the edge of the mattress. "Okay, spill it, Marla," she croaked. "Where's Sean in all this mess? What doesn't Ethan want me to know?"

Marla grinned. "Actually, I'm giddy to be the one to tell you. After the ambulance left—and I swore Ethan was going to start running after it like a dog to be with you—Sean was shaking and

THE NEIGHBOR'S SECRET

mumbling like some crazy person. I think he thought you were dead. That he'd killed you."

Allie couldn't stop a smile from creeping across her lips.

"Ethan came unglued. He actually arrived at the fry shack and heard you two arguing. Then the whole place went up—never seen anything blow so fast. It was *frightening.* Your mother was weeping and wailing, your father looked like he'd died when he saw you stretched out on the lawn . . . and, well, Ethan marched up to Sean and punched him right in the face."

"What!?"

"That's right, honey."

"Did Sean hit him back?"

"Nope. His nose started bleeding and he was lurching around, yelling about the pain like the self-centered prig he is, while *you* were being carried into the ambulance, for heaven's sake."

Allie fell back to the bed in shock. *Ethan had punched Sean.* "Then what happened?"

"Your father told Sean to leave Heartland Cove and never come back. Sean said he was already packed and had only come to tell you goodbye—until you followed him back to Toronto."

Allie snorted and pushed herself to a standing position, one hand on the bathroom door frame. "I'll bet that made my father furious."

"That doesn't even begin to describe it. He told Sean that the next time he saw his daughter would be over his dead body."

Air whooshed out of Allie's chest. "Wow! Go Dad!"

"Wish I had a father like yours, honey. He's the best."

When Allie dressed, she tried not to cringe at the wide bandage on her right thigh. It was bigger than she expected and extremely tender. She hoped a prescription for more pain meds was on docket.

Marla had wisely brought a sundress for her so Allie didn't have to pull slacks or jeans over her leg.

"Need any help with that hand they wrapped up like a mummy?" Marla called through the door.

"Think I got it," Allie answered. She opened the door and stepped back into the room. "Just tie up the laces in back and help me buckle my sandals."

The dress was cool, the cotton hem flowing below her knees and hiding the bulky wrappings. Walking felt strange, as if she'd grown an elephant's leg. A wheelchair was brought to take her downstairs to the exit.

"Ethan's outside the door waiting for you," Marla reassured her with a wink.

"Cut it out, Marla," Allie said, but her stomach jumped at the knowledge of Ethan being here. Holding her hand in the hospital bed. Punching out Sean. Coming to her rescue. Defending her. Telling her he was falling for her—just before she yelled at him to take his stuff and get out of the house. He was kind and considerate and she'd been a jerk to him.

She closed her eyes as she settled into the wheelchair. She was probably just tired and not in her right mind. Benjamin Ethan Miles (Smith) warmed her, thrilled her, and scared her all at the same time. The thought of having him in her life was such a complete opposite experience from what had happened with her relationship with Sean.

At first, she'd been excited about the lawyer, his intellect and confidence, but after knowing Ethan just a few weeks she realized that Sean had dominated their life together. It hadn't been a partnership. He'd dismissed her ideas and prolonged their engagement until he couldn't any longer.

It was a sobering realization to know that he'd only agreed to marry her because she kept demanding it. His heart had not been in it, which begged the question of whether Sean had ever planned to be standing at the altar watching her enter the church all dressed in white.

The ache in her throat swelled. That knowledge still hurt, but

THE NEIGHBOR'S SECRET

perhaps Sean had actually done her a favor. How could she be happy with someone who married her because he felt obligated rather than truly committed to their life together?

Ethan Smith wanted her in ways Sean never had.

"I've got all your paperwork," Marla told her. "Let's rock-and-roll."

Allie squinted at the bright sunshine when the double glass hospital doors silently opened. Ethan was there, gazing at her, his eyes on her face, relief in his expression.

He lifted her up as though she weighed nothing and then carried her to the passenger's side of his car. His warm hands were on the bare skin of her back and a jolt of electricity ran through her entire body. She held onto the handle, suddenly unsteady. Her body screamed for more Ethan. For his hands to be everywhere.

"Hey, you okay?" he asked gently.

"Yep, I'm good," she said, settling into the seat cushion and trying to hide the flush rushing up her neck.

It was so good to be outside, to feel like a normal person rather than a patient. Allie touched at the bandage on her arm where the IV had been and the wrist band she needed to cut off. "I'm a little nervous to go home," she admitted. "The morbid part of me wants to open up the bandage and see how bad it is underneath."

"Don't look until you see the doctor again in a couple days. I don't want you fainting—especially if I'm not around to catch you."

She gave him a tremulous smile, her palms suddenly sweaty. "You're probably right."

The leather seats were luxurious and plush, the vehicle loaded with every conceivable upgrade and gadget, and Ethan had turned on all the comfort controls for the drive back to Heartland.

Marla shut the car door, calling out, "See you two later. I'm off to work."

"I can still help you with the business," Allie told her.

"Not right now, sweetie." And Marla was gone.

Allie stared through the windshield while Ethan turned over the engine. This was the first time they'd been alone since their argument and the sudden silence felt palpable.

Ethan smoothly pulled into traffic and two blocks later there was a red light. When he braked, he turned toward her. "I hope this isn't uncomfortable for you. I know we ended on bad terms. And I regret pushing you."

"What do you mean "pushing me"—in what way?"

"I was giving you all sorts of unsolicited advice about your feelings, your anger, and your fiancé—"

"—ex-fiancé," Allie clarified.

"I was wrong to do that. I'm sorry."

"It's been a bad month."

Ethan let out a low whistle. "That's the understatement of the year."

Allie took a slow breath, knowing she had to say something. Wanting to say it. She tried to brush aside the awkwardness she'd felt ever since she saw him at her bedside, after their horrible argument two days ago. "Thank you for saving my life, Ethan."

He shrugged, minimizing his rescue. "You were on your way out of the building. There were dozens of people around to help."

"I overheard one of the nurses say I got out in the nick of time. That the roof collapsed seconds later. You were the one that shoved me to the ground, weren't you? To drop and roll and put out the flames on my clothing. You kept talking to me so I wouldn't pass out. I remember now."

"Seeing your apron in flames—the shock and pain on your face—that was one of the hardest things I've ever had to witness."

"Um, I also got your text message Saturday night even though I never responded. I appreciated the sentiments, the apology, and the no pressure. All of it. I never told you."

"You didn't have to. I meant what I said. It's up to you where we go from here, Allie. I'll stay, I'll walk away. I'll leave you alone for as long as you need to figure things out. Especially while you heal from this terrible accident."

"The Victorian house is still mine? Rent free until September first?"

Ethan lightly touched her cheek. "Good grief, Allie, the house is yours for as long as you need it."

"I'd offer you your room back—" she began.

Ethan shook his head. "No. You need time and space to heal. Physically and emotionally. I know losing Sean has been killing you. And, like I told you several days ago, it's been killing me to have you so close, and yet so far."

His words were both a comfort and a thrill, but Allie remained silent while Ethan maneuvered around traffic onto Highway 130, then onto Somerville Road to cross back over the Heartland Bridge.

She gave a small laugh. "I have to admit it felt so good to yell at Sean. To tell him to leave forever."

"Do you regret that last part?" There was hesitancy in Ethan's voice.

Allie shook her head, cradling the bandaged hand in her good one. "I'm surprised at how relieved I feel. How light, actually, like a huge burden has suddenly lifted. Well, except for my right leg that I swear turned into an elephant leg with this thick bandage." She turned to him. "I've been realizing how much Sean controlled my life and my emotions. Our relationship always had to be on his terms."

"That's a lot of big stuff to come to understand."

Allie's fingers tightened around the door handle. She tried to put into words the insight she was finally grasping. "Guess I'm a slow learner. You were right. I've been afraid of moving forward. Hanging onto hope that I wasn't wrong about Sean being a complete jerk. I was stuck in neutral and too anxious to do anything about it."

Ethan touched her hand gently. "I'm not going to rub it in," he said with a glint in his eye. "But I'm ecstatic to hear you say that."

A mile later, he turned to take the road into Heartland Cove. The hills turned familiar and beloved, as the blue of the river water came into view. "It really is picturesque coming in this direction, isn't it?" Ethan said. "The covered bridge with the Victorian town as a backdrop."

"I love this view, too," Allie agreed. "Charming, striking, and scenic all rolled into one. Too bad we had to make a run to the hospital to enjoy it."

Without thinking, Allie nudged his arm with hers and laughed, then quickly pulled away when her heart leaped at the connection between them. His skin was warm and heady, his entire presence tugged at her like a magnet.

"Hey," Ethan said. "I think you know by now that I don't bite."

"Biting isn't what I'm afraid of."

Ethan pulled into the driveway and parked, his hands still on the steering wheel. "You don't have to be afraid of anything with me. And that's a promise."

She stared into his rich silky brown eyes and her breath caught. She could get lost in those eyes. They were gentle, compassionate. Not the snapping, jumpy nervous eyes of Sean Carter.

"I need to get the lawnmower out and do some mowing," Ethan finally said.

He was speaking and Allie could hear him, but she could only stare at his lips, wanting to know if that day on the beach—that kiss—was merely an anomaly and not actually real.

"That scraggly lawn is suddenly looking Amazon jungle-like," he went on when she didn't respond.

She cleared her throat. "Don't people like you have gardeners?"

"People like me?" He cocked an eyebrow at her.

"Sorry, that was bad, but you know what I mean. For example, Sean would never do yard work. And he isn't wealthy in the slightest—at least not yet."

"It doesn't bother me to get my hands dirty. I like exploring the world, even the grubby parts. No stuffy offices—unless it's a storage unit filled with history."

Allie smiled. "Miss Ellie's historical society project."

Their gaze broke apart when Ethan opened the door and climbed out, heading around to open her car door. "Let's get you inside. You need to lie on the couch and watch chick movies for a few days and take a lot of naps."

"Luxury! Do I get chocolate, too?"

"Only Laura Secord Chocolates. And only in small doses, my girl."

CHAPTER 19

Ethan was true to his word. He brought a stack of movies —all the romantic comedies she craved, plus Jane Austen's BBC productions. He made a point of providing Laura Secord chocolates for her to devour while she perfected the art of lazy. Plus Ethan made her dinner every night.

Her family came to visit that first night she was home, too.

Surprisingly, Erin burst into tears and threw her arms around her neck. "I thought you died!"

"You can't get rid of me that easily." Allie hugged her back, and it felt so good to squeeze her baby sister after weeks of being annoyed with her. Knowing how close she'd come to losing Erin, as well as how frightened Ethan had been, was very sobering for Allie. All because of Sean's selfish actions.

When Dad put his arms around her, he whispered in her ear, "I'm sorry for not telling Sean to get lost sooner."

"It's not your fault, Dad. I feel more badly about you losing the business. What are you going to do?"

"Buildings heal faster than people do, sweetie," he said. He seemed to search her face for any lingering trauma and Allie smiled at him to reassure him that she was perfectly fine.

THE NEIGHBOR'S SECRET

"I'll be good as new in a few weeks."

"Well, I have good news, too. Our dear town has already come together and they've decided to hold a barn-raising just like in the good old days. Instead of a barn, we're rebuilding the fry shop and enlarging it from a truck to a small, portable shop on a trailer. This coming weekend I take the original building plans to the city commissioner's office. Blake Howard is going to act as foreman of the job."

Allie's jaw dropped. "That's fantastic. I always complained about this tiny little town in the middle of nowhere, but right now it's as good as gold. But how will you pay for all the materials? The cost is going to be triple what you originally bought it for."

"Howard said that there will be some fundraisers to help us out—until the insurance money kicks in, which could take months."

Allie threw her arms around her father's neck. "I'm so happy, Dad. You deserve every good thing. Thank you for sticking with me and all my bad decisions."

The lines around his mouth deepened as he scrutinized her face. "Life's a learning process, honey. We've all had our share of licks and wounds and idiocy."

"Ooh, touché—and ouch. That last part was brilliant, Dad."

"I do my best," he answered with a wink.

"Okay, you two, out of my way," Mom said, pushing forward to embrace her daughter. "Thank God the doctors say you're going to heal completely. No scarring," she added, fighting tears.

"Don't cry. I'm really going to be fine. I'm not even having fire nightmares."

"Well, you've been sedated," Mrs. Strickland said.

"Phoebe," her husband warned.

She made a face and suddenly Allie knew where she got the bad habit from. "Honestly Mom, except for some bruising and stinging around the burn areas, the sleeping pills work really well. Sean is gone. I'm done. For good. And the feeling is so freeing, I can't even tell you."

"I never thought I'd hear you say that. Ethan Smith was amazing. He was so brave running—no, *sprinting*—into the burning truck to rescue you."

"You mean the place was already on fire? I thought it happened after I ran out."

"He's our hero." Mrs. Strickland lowered her voice, "And here I've been thinking he was taking advantage of you living here the past month."

"He pays all the bills, Mother. He owns the house. And because of the rental agreement mix-up I get the house for nothing until September first. You could say I'm taking advantage of his generosity."

Of course, there was the whole break-in to her bathroom on that first night. If she'd had a .22 rifle in the shower, Ethan Smith might have been carried out on a stretcher, but she wasn't going to tell her parents that. Instead, Allie smiled sweetly.

"You know there are other ways to take advantage of a young girl," her mother went on.

"I'm a woman, Mom. And Ethan has never been anything but a perfect gentleman. In every way."

"If you say so, dear."

Just then, Ethan returned to the front room with drinks for everyone and raised his glass to toast Allie's health and recovery. There were cheers and Allie narrowed her eyes to glare at him. She sidled closer. "You know I want to punch you in the arm good and hard."

He grinned. "I'm looking forward to it. Arm wrestle? I'll even let you use your un-burned arm."

"You're impossible."

"I know."

Allie sat back down on the couch, frowning as she realized

THE NEIGHBOR'S SECRET

that she and Sean had never bantered like this. She'd never had any real fun with her uptight lawyer fiancé.

~

TWO WEEKS LATER, after several doctor appointments, fresh bandages, a dozen movies, and five pounds of chocolates, Allie was healing much better than she'd expected.

Now she was getting restless after being cooped up when the summer weather was currently so perfect.

Ethan had been off doing mysterious things the last several days so Allie decided to go exploring on her own. The doctor had given permission to drive herself anywhere she wanted.

A little sleuthing trip had been on her to-do list before the fire, and now she was more eager than ever to learn Ethan's final secret.

When she pulled away from the house and drove down the street, she felt like a teenager cutting school. The freedom was euphoric. But, while sitting at the next red light, a sudden pang ran through her, like being stabbed in the gut. A realization that left her gulping air.

Ever since the fire, Sean hadn't sent a single message to see if she had come through alive. Not a phone call, text message, or get well card. What a sniveling coward. Worse than that, the silence showed his true, despicable character.

Tears burned at the corner of her eye. "I almost married a man who never truly loved me."

He'd run off when the fry shack caught on fire, scared at what he'd done, and with no thought other than for himself. The world revolved around Sean Carter. That was the plain and simple fact.

It would be easy to let that knowledge eat her up inside. Six weeks ago, it would have wreaked havoc on her mental state, but as Allie sped through the green light she determined not to be Sean's victim any longer.

He'd done her a *favor* by not showing up for the wedding. She had dodged a bullet.

A magazine of AK47 bullets.

∼

THE MORNING SUN was a halo of burning beauty. Heartland Cove had never looked prettier. Fresh summer paint and swept streets always made things cheerful. Even it if was partly a show for the tourists.

As usual, Jane Austen and Laura Secord chocolates had been a wonder cure.

In the past when she heard people from outside New Brunswick talk about how quaint and old-fashioned Heartland Cove was, it had usually made Allie bristle. Not anymore. She was lucky to live here. It was like stepping back into the past. Despite its quirks and blemishes and secret billionaires, the town was enchanting and the people had hearts of gold.

The fry shack raising had been extraordinarily successful. After two solid days of thirty neighbors and friends working, the new portable shop was framed in, insulated, and sheet-rocked.

When Allie drove past she could see electricians and plumbers going in for the next stage of construction.

The previous night her father had said that the taping, texturing and painting was going to be done by their neighbor, Mr. Lane, who had offered his services.

Today her parents were shopping for linoleum and new appliances: fryers, sinks, and stoves. Thankfully, the cash register had been saved and the heavy black thing was like a battle-scarred ship—blackened by smoke, but with the contents intact.

Not having the fry shack open had given Allie these weeks to recover, but she was going stir-crazy despite helping Marla with the photo mounting. A bit tricky with her bum hand, but she was learning to maneuver despite it. Mostly, the only fingers bandaged up were her fourth and fifth fingers and today was the last day to wear any sort of bandage. The doctor wanted the hand to air heal now.

Allie was still wearing skirts so she didn't have to slide jeans up over her burned leg. The pain was mostly gone, despite the fact that her skin still had a dark pink hue.

After passing the Wesleyan church, Allie took a narrow road that led up into the hills. It was deeply forested and the trees were magnificent.

A flutter went off in her stomach. She was fairly certain this was the road Marla had said was the location where Ethan was working on his refurbishment of an old, abandoned house, but she sincerely hoped he wasn't there right now. She didn't want him to think she was spying on him.

But she was bored. And she was curious.

A quarter of a mile later, there was a big white sign:

**Future Site of the Heartland Cove County Historical Preservation Society.
Opening Next Summer!**

"What new secret is this?" Allie said aloud. "I thought you were remodeling a new residence for yourself, Ethan Smith."

Up ahead through the pines and silver birch Allie thought she spotted a structure, but it was hard to see through the dense forest.

A quick peek and she'd head back home before Ethan ever saw her.

Allie parked the car, slowly pulling off the asphalt road into a little alcove behind the construction site sign. Easing one leg out at a time, she stood and quietly shut the car door.

The air was perfectly still. Birds twittered above her and

sunlight dappled the leaves, painting the forest floor. A leaf fluttered down, hitting her hair and then dropping to the dirt. The ground felt mossy and damp with so little daylight coming through.

While Allie walked forward, the building came into view. It was situated in a small clearing, tall trees strategically left for shade around the perimeter and rear gardens.

A partial lawn desperately needed cutting. The rear property was filled with lumber, stacks of sheet rock, sawhorses and power tools. The local hardware store was obviously getting a lot of business between this project and her parents' rebuilding.

Ethan didn't appear to be on the premises. She'd poke around for a few minutes and then leave before he returned.

Moving closer, Allie realized that the old house was almost completely gutted. The gabled roofline and gingerbread Victorian portico was intact, only needing a fresh coat of paint and some trim repair work, but the interior was a different story.

The structure was two levels with a circular dining room and a matching tower directly above. The old home must have been large and magnificent when first built, owned by some rich founder more than a hundred years ago.

At the front entrance, Allie could see that there was a splendid staircase curving up to the second floor despite all the other walls having been torn down. So Ethan was going to keep the spectacular hardwood stairs. Wise decision.

The open balcony overlooked the downstairs. What a view that was going to be.

In her mind's eye, Allie could picture the stately rooms reformed. The parquet floors. The columns and front desk. Displays of Heartland's history. Items salvaged from residents' attics, polished and preserved under glassed-in walnut cases.

"It's going to be beautiful," she breathed.

A noise caught her off guard, but it wasn't the sound of a car.

Maybe a mouse scurrying through on its way to its home in the field behind the property.

The sound came again, an odd crunching. This time infinitely louder than a mouse's tiny rustlings.

She moved forward to look out the back windows which were still open to the outdoors. Her heart went into high gear, banging against her ribs so hard she couldn't breathe. "Oh, Lord, oh Lord, oh, Lord," she whispered hoarsely.

A gigantic moose had come from out of nowhere and was roaming the perimeter of the house, stopping every few seconds to nibble at the trim along the roofline.

She hadn't seen a moose all summer. Dad had said it had been a quiet year for wandering, lost moose. When she was in high school, one had come right down Main Street, its fearsome horns and gigantic head swiveling about terrorizing everyone.

Shoppers had crouched in store doorways and cars turned down side streets to avoid it. Then the moose had walked across the river to the other side and disappeared into the forest.

Of course, her classmates had dared each other to go out and try to grab its attention to see what it would do. Just to tease the animal.

But they'd been stupid. Dad had put the fear of these mammoth-sized animals in Allie when she was just beginning to toddle around—warning her and her siblings every few months to stay far away from the creatures. If provoked, a seven-foot tall male weighing more than a thousand pounds could charge a human and crush him in minutes.

This one was about twenty paces away, butting its head against the porch soffits. The horns were outrageously frightening. If the animal wanted to, it could walk right through the bare doorways and sweep her off her feet in seconds.

"I have to hide," she hissed to herself, eyes darting about. Backing up slowly, Allie tried not to trip over building paraphernalia and rotted floorboards as she moved in the opposite direction of the animal as it circled the house.

A minute later, she realized that she was trapped. Too far from the staircase, and too far from the front door. The double entrance with its oversized opening for a pair of grand stained-glass doors was tall enough for the moose to walk right in and make itself at home. And it probably would.

CHAPTER 20

Frustration gurgled in her throat. She fumbled in her skirt pocket for her cell phone, but remembered that she'd left it in the car with her purse. Five minutes—that's all she had planned on being here.

But what she had forgotten was that her keys were in that left pocket and now they jangled loudly in the quiet house. The noise made tears burn her eyes. Could she outrun the monster?

She tried to remember everything she knew about moose, but her mind was blank. She'd lived in the city for far too long.

A hand suddenly pressed against the pocket where she gripped the keys to keep them from rattling. Allie let out a yelp—quickly cut short when a second hand came around her shoulder and covered her mouth.

Terror crawled up her throat, but Ethan's voice came into her ear. "I got you, Allie. Stay perfectly still."

She twisted in his arms with relief, trying not to gasp out loud when he uncovered her mouth.

He put a finger to his lips, motioning her to follow him down a short hallway. "There's a window in this side room. We'll crawl through and head back to your car."

"Won't he chase us?"

"He's busy eating now, but coming closer to the front door. I really need to get the place enclosed and the new roof installed before it rains again."

She gaped at him, smiling tremulously. "Obviously you believe we're going to survive this moose encounter and live."

He grinned, slipping his hand down her arm and gripping her fingers tightly in his. "Of course, we're going to survive. It's the anticipation of kissing you again that I'm dying from."

Despite her fear, it had not gone unnoticed to Allie that Ethan was wearing jeans slung low around his hips, but no shirt. His chest was more chiseled and muscled than Allie had expected for a rich guy who ran around taking pictures. The guy must work out at a gym. Dang, he looked good. She felt her temperature rise and her cheeks go hot.

"Are you okay?" Ethan whispered against her hair.

He had her close up against him to reduce the noise they made as they moved through the house. She nodded, sure that he could feel her heart stuttering inside her chest.

But the adrenaline rush wasn't just the moose. It was Ethan looking so fine, so perfect.

Had she ever been turned on like this with Sean? She must have been, but Allie couldn't remember. She couldn't remember anything beyond the feel of Ethan's warm skin against her arm, his hand tight in hers.

At the moment, she'd have followed him anywhere. With sudden clarity, Allie knew that she trusted Ethan implicitly. It was a very surprising thought.

He wouldn't hurt her. She knew deep down in the core of his soul that he was a good person.

Quickly, he swung his legs up onto the window sill and then reached back and lifted her through. Allie swiveled her hips, tucking her feet in tightly to get through the small space and then jumped lightly to the ground while Ethan finished coming through. Once he'd landed her quietly onto the dirt, he held her close for a moment, assessing where the moose was located.

"You can let me go now, you know."

He smiled. "What if I don't want to?"

"I can run faster on my own two feet. So can you."

"In those sandals?"

For an answer, Allie slipped them off and dangled them from her fingers. "Just point me to the track and I'll get there before you know it."

Ethan swore softly. "Dumb animal is inside the house now. I hope he doesn't smash all my tools."

"Hopefully he'll get bored and leave soon."

"Not too soon because this is our chance to run."

"Where are we running to? Do you have a car here?"

"My work truck is on the opposite side of the house. Your car is a lot closer. That's my suggestion unless you want to climb a tree."

"Very funny." If his truck was on the far side of the construction site, that explained why Allie hadn't seen it. She jerked the keys from her pocket and took off at a sprint, the hem of her dress flying around her knees, cool grass under her toes.

Ethan kept pace, arms pumping, throwing a few grins her direction as they ran.

She widened her eyes. "This isn't a joke!" she shrieked. "We're escaping a freaking moose!"

"But you have to admit it is sort of funny," he yelled back.

Running at top speed, two seconds later they approached her Pontiac. Allie pressed the button on her keys to unlock the doors, jerked open the passenger door, and tossed the keys to Ethan. "You drive, I'm too nervous. I've never had to outrun a moose while in a car."

"It's easy. Watch."

The engine roared and Ethan peeled down the narrow asphalt. "We're going to turn this into a better road, too," he told her. "For all those thousands of patrons we'll be having next summer. Maybe even paint dotted white stripes down the middle."

Allie shook her head and laughed. "You don't seem too upset about a moose in your house."

"At least it's a gutted house right now. He can't do too much damage. Except for that new power saw I just bought."

A minute later, Ethan reached the main road and then pulled off into a stand of trees. "Pretty sure we lost him," he said, glancing furtively behind them.

Allie laughed. "I think you're laughing at me."

"Nope." Ethan's face was serious. He glanced down at the floor of the car and Allie was glad it was clean and not embarrassingly cluttered. "But you do have the prettiest toes."

She glanced at her pink painted toenails with the little stars and laughed at his serious expression. "Oh, honestly! Hey, I have to do something while I'm watching *Pride and Prejudice* so I'm partially productive during my recuperation. And *why* aren't you clothed?" she blurted out. "I don't normally see construction guys half-dressed. And you're missing your tool belt, aren't you?"

"I was up in the attic laying insulation and doing my best not to fall through the ceiling until the heat got to me. I came down the back stairs and took my shirt off to soak it in cold water with every intention of putting it back. Poor man's air conditioning. Then I heard footsteps. I'd hoped it wasn't one of the inspectors, but instead there you were. As if I'd conjured you up from my dreams. But when I saw that moose right behind you I figured my life was worth a shirt. At least temporarily."

Allie felt her lips quirk as she tried not to smile broadly at him. "I can't believe you lay your own insulation."

"Don't you know it builds character?"

"Oh, is that where you found yours—up in the attic?" Allie grinned at him, but curiosity won out over the questions of Ethan as a construction worker. "I saw the sign. When did your new house become the new headquarters of the Heartland Cove County Historical Society? Your grandmother said it was disbanded when the former president died."

"It was for a few months, but my grandmother is currently president. She stepped in so that the two-hundred-year history of Heartland Cove wasn't lost."

Allie's head spun. "Okay, but you lost me! I thought you were building a house."

"I didn't actually say that a few weeks ago. My grandmother wanted the building of an actual historical center kept on the down low, so to speak."

"Actually, I can imagine your grandmother saying that," Allie said with a smile. "'Keep this on the down low, Benjamin Ethan Miles. And that's an order.'"

Ethan laughed out loud, then his expression softened as he gazed at her, morning light streaming through the car windows.

"The historical society of the last few decades was never very organized—and never an official entity. Just a few descendants of the original settlers meeting in their living rooms. They had no place to store documents, display old photos, or archive the town's history. My grandmother urged me to renovate this decrepit old house and move forward as quickly as we could before she's not here any longer. She has entire airtight storerooms filled with archival material and photos from the past two hundred years."

Allie swept her hand through the air, pointing to the construction site. "So the story about the incoming highway flattening the town, and the controversy over the bridge, is merely a cover for this new site?"

Ethan gave a true laugh then. "No, the historical society is a cover for my investigation into Mayor Jefferies mischief."

"Being a photographer is the perfect cover for both."

"We hope to have the house turned into a museum by the end of next summer so we're moving fast. Grandmother's cronies meet almost daily to sift through the boxes in storage. About two hundred of them."

"That's a staggering task."

"Monumental."

Ethan shifted, reaching out to brush a hand against her cheek. "You okay, Miss Allie Strickland? After the moose scare, that is."

Actually, Allie's nerves were on fire. The look Ethan was giving her was making her head whirl and her heart stammer. She was cold and hot all at once.

When she leaned forward to turn the AC up a notch, Ethan's arms slid around her shoulders and he brought her toward him. "I just want to feel your heartbeat go crazy again," he said softly.

Ethan's day-old stubble brushed against her face and Allie's pulse went into high gear.

His voice was rough and yet tender. "You feel absolutely fantastic, Allie. Now put your arms around me."

"Is that an order?"

"Times ten, you gorgeous girl."

Without speaking, Allie's hands moved up his bare chest and she tried not to gasp. His skin was warm and he smelled spicy, like autumn pumpkins. Then her arms went around the back of his neck and her cheek was pressed against his.

Ethan lowered his head, and his lips were suddenly on hers, soft, gentle, making her breath catch.

"The gear shift," Allie murmured, not wanting to break away.

"Damn the gear shift, I've wanted to kiss you again for a long time."

"But it's digging into my hip."

His hand went down her side and Ethan squeezed the curve of her waist. Allie felt as if she was on fire. The feel of his bare skin was scrambling her brain, sending shock waves through her entire body and soul.

Their kiss deepened and Ethan's lips tasted perfect.

"I'm losing my mind," she whispered. "I think I'm going to laugh and cry and start hyperventilating all at the same time."

"Then it's time to stop, my love."

They broke apart and Allie gazed up into his eyes, her arms still locked around his neck. He wasn't laughing at her. He was dead serious.

"This is too fast," she whispered, not wanting this feeling to end, but knowing she had to sit up, go home, and figure out her head.

Amusement played over his face. "It's been almost two months, Miss Strickland. Have we given our chaperone the slip?"

"You know what I mean. I can't get into a serious relationship without knowing—without, I don't know—" she broke off, unable to put into words what she was feeling.

Ethan's biceps flexed as he helped her sit up again in her seat, brushing the hair out of her eyes with the back of his hand. "I know exactly what you mean. What's happening between us is too big. It's not a fling. I'm serious about you. About doing this right."

Allie bit at her lips, reaching down to clasp his hand. "That's it exactly. I have to know it's not me rebounding or just being lonely. My ego being starved after—after. Well, you know. I don't even want to say his name."

"That's a good sign, I think." Ethan gave her a tender smile. He wasn't jealous at all. He was confident in himself, and in her.

Allie gazed through the windshield. Not a single car had passed since they had pulled over. It felt as though they were the only two people in the world. "I keep having these epiphanies about Sean and about myself. Thank you for understanding, for not pressuring me."

Ethan looked thoughtful. "You know, when I was a kid, I used to visit my grandmother during Christmas break. I'd see you playing in the snow with the other kids on the sledding hill near her house."

Allie turned to him. "Wait a minute. Did your grandmother Ellie used to live in that huge Victorian at the edge of the river? It's all coming to me now."

"Yep, that was her. We had this fancy catered Christmas dinner while all I wanted to do was play with my new train set. Or ride my new bike. Or whatever it was. When I was a senior in high school I used to daydream about walking along the bridge holding your hand."

Allie's brain whirled at the unexpected confession. "No way!"

A tinge of red crept up Ethan's neck. "It's true. I'd have this crazy movie running in my head of holding your hand while we strolled inside the bridge at midnight when nobody was around. I wanted to kiss you, but midnight was a good time because then you wouldn't be able to see my red, embarrassed face."

"Oh, Ethan." Allie brushed her fingers over his chin.

Ethan gave a small shudder of pleasure and picked up her hand, kissing the center of her palm. "Yes, I was a complete geek. It was the best daydream I ever had." He turned his full brown eyes on her. "But you know what?"

"What?" Allie asked, her voice soft.

"Kissing you for real is even better than my level ten best daydream."

CHAPTER 21

"I'll drive you back up to the house," Allie told him a moment later.

"Oh, man, you're going to make me go back to work?"

"Even heirs to mind-boggling fortunes must pretend to work."

"Hey! I haven't inherited anything yet, my girl. I have to work to pay for my groceries. But after unexpectedly seeing you, I'm not sure I can focus on working any more today. I just want to get a picnic basket and lay my head in your lap."

"I suppose I'll feed you grapes?" Allie said, amused.

Ethan laughed. "Something like that. Pretty sexist, eh?"

Allie felt an odd jump in her stomach, and sat up straighter. "Or sexy."

Ethan smacked his head back against the bucket seat headrest. "Good grief, woman, you'd better stop that kind of talk right now."

"Sorry." Allie tried to look contrite, but not too much. He was easy to tease. "But I do think you need your shirt on to head back into town."

"True." He started up the car again and pulled back onto the drive toward the construction site. "Looks like the moose is gone."

Allie peered through the windshield. "Are you sure?"

"If he was still in there I'd probably see a smashed wall on the ground. He was probably curious and exploring and then headed back to his mate in the woods."

"I hope so." Allie shivered, the air conditioning cold on her bare arms. "I saw your sign when I pulled in. Next summer to open is ambitious. Do you think you'll be ready? An official, public Heartland Cove Historical Society center is a huge undertaking."

Ethan nodded, about to slide out of the car to come around and open her door. "Stay right where you are."

Allie began to protest. "I can open my own door."

"I know you're fully capable, but it's a small gesture to show you how much I respect you." He laughed at himself, sitting back down in the driver's seat. "Wow, that sounded stiff and pompous. It just shows how much I want to do for you. A way to demonstrate the love I'm feeling."

Allie gulped. How could he speak of love? "Surely you're joking? Being deferential."

She glanced away because she was staring at his six-pack abs way too much.

Ethan spoke quietly, staring out the windshield. "My parents met and were married within two months. You and I are already coming up on that."

"Two months," Allie echoed, astonished at how fast time was going. "Your parents are crazy!" she added with a burst of laughter.

"Maybe, but even though they were married fewer than fifteen years before my mother died, I think it was a happy fifteen years. And," he paused, glancing up at her, "I think we're getting to know each other pretty well."

Allie went silent, staring at him. She loved gazing at him,

actually. She loved his smile, his manners, his honesty, his refreshing candor.

Sean was always working some sort of deal, barreling through life, talking too much through a nice dinner out, restless during intermission at a play or show, and then rushing back to work before she had a chance to really talk to him. Or even a chance to breathe.

"I know it's fast, and I'll stop talking about it. I'm sure it makes you uncomfortable."

"Not exactly," Allie said, but she didn't know how to explain what she was feeling, except that her heart raced like a shot of adrenaline whenever he was near and her mind overflowed with every thought of him.

Ethan reached for her hand, interlocking their fingers. "It's okay. We'll take it one step at a time. And if you want me to bugger off, just tell me, but if those kisses in the car are any indication . . ." his voice trailed off meaningfully.

"Am I so easy to read?"

"Not really, but you were—are—hot."

"It's the humidity. The sun. The moose."

Ethan's grin was slow—he didn't believe her excuses for a minute.

"It's—it's—I can't explain it. Too much has happened."

"You're recovering. From the fire, and, dare I mention him who shouldn't be named—Sean Carter?"

A laugh bubbled up her throat. "I thought a lot about him while changing bandages. Changing DVDs. I thought a lot about how he took advantage of our relationship. He made assumptions. And he turned out to be a Class A jerk. He left me to die in my own parent's shop. Okay, I'm probably exaggerating, but not by much."

Ethan's jaw clenched. He got out of the car, slammed the door, and then sprinted around to help her out.

Stepping close, he wrapped his arms around her shoulders.

For a moment they stood there, together, without speaking. "He would never have been there for you and your marriage," Ethan stated in a low voice.

"Here's the funny part," she admitted. "Yesterday I realized that I was relieved Sean was gone. It was so freeing to know that I never have to deal with him, or speak to him, or put up with his BS ever again."

Allie put her chin into his neck, squeezing her eyes against the sudden emotion.

"I am so glad to hear you say that," he whispered.

After a moment they broke apart, but Ethan's grip remained tight on her hand. "You want to come inside and see the artist's renderings of the new historical society? I'm bidding out some of the work, of course, and I've got a couple of buddies who do construction in Montreal who are coming out in a month before winter hits. I even promised to pay them."

Allie bumped his shoulder. "That's generous."

"My grandmother is putting up the front money so that helps."

"Which means you, too, actually."

Ethan shrugged. "I guess so. I want her to see her long-time dream come to fruition before she—before she's gone. In many ways, she's been like a mother to me."

Allie pressed his fingers, gazing up into his pensive face and knowing that the thought of Miss Ellie's passing was not something he wanted to think about, despite her age.

"Come inside and let me walk you through the place."

"I'd love to, but it's pretty lonely and deserted out here. . ." Allie's voice trailed away.

"Are you afraid to be alone with me?"

"No!" Allie said, and then laughed. The protest had come out much stronger than she intended. "I wasn't expecting to see you out here at all."

"Aha! You were spying on me, then. The truth comes out."

THE NEIGHBOR'S SECRET

Allie turned away to hide her blush. "I'm a citizen of Heartland," she said primly. "And I wanted to know what the new historical society location looked like."

"You're suddenly interested in the back-story of this speck on the map?"

"I've spent the last seven years far away. It's true I couldn't wait to get out of Heartland. Living in Toronto was exciting and fun—horrible grad school notwithstanding—but I have to admit it's nice to be home. The frantic pace was getting to me."

"Maybe it was the company you were keeping."

"Touché. And just for the record, you're terrible."

"So let it be written."

Ethan's cell rang. He glanced at the number and then said, "Excuse me."

Turning away, he walked off several paces and then answered. First he listened and then responded in brief words, mostly yes and no.

Allie had the feeling Ethan was trying not to reveal the conversation. Why was he keeping secrets again?

"Glad to hear it," Ethan said. "Better than expected. Okay, talk to you later."

He hung up and lifted his head. The sun was bronzing his fine chest and Allie bit her lips to keep from rushing him.

"So?" she asked when he pocketed the cell phone into the front of his jeans.

At first Ethan tried to act as though he didn't understand her question. "Oh, that? The phone call? Just the lumber yard about my—a—project order. No big deal. Come on."

Allie stared at the tall stacks of 2x6 pieces of lumber and trusses to repair the roof's sagging middle, all sitting in neat piles on both sides of the construction site.

The man wasn't telling her the truth. Or at least, not all of it. It reminded her of those first few days when she learned he was using an alias. When she suspected he was in cahoots with the mayor over the highway.

The cold feeling in her belly returned and she tugged against him, pleading with her eyes for him to tell her what was going on. Why was he being evasive when he was so open about everything else?

Finally, she said, "I promised Marla to help her with a wedding this evening and we need to prep for it."

"Marla gets the benefit of my misfortune." Ethan cast a pair of puppy dog eyes at her.

"You'll survive," Allie told him, not knowing whether to be irritated or not. Was the conversation so private he couldn't just tell her? What was so secretive about a lumber order?

Ethan came forward and Allie knew he was hoping for a kiss goodbye.

"I think you've had enough kissing for one afternoon," she told him.

He shook his hair out of his eyes. "I can never get enough of you."

Allie drove back home, unsettled. Was she getting in over her head with Ethan? One moment he was rich, the next he was poor. He was a photographer. No, he owned a construction company. One moment he was Ethan Smith, the next he was Benjamin Ethan Miles the III, grandson to the richest family in Heartland Cove.

Marla was waiting for her at the house when she arrived.

"Who have you been kissing?" her friend asked, giving her a sly look.

"That's ridiculous," Allie said, tossing her purse onto one of the sofas. Her cell phone slipped onto the floor and she picked it up, plus a lip gloss that had clattered out. "What are you talking about?"

"You look like a cat that swallowed a mouse—"

"You mean a canary."

"You just have that *look* like when we were at university and you'd come home flushed and embarrassed to admit you'd been making out with your date."

"Stop being so astute," Allie said with a glare.

"Ethan Smith. That's all I have to say." Marla pulled her into the darkroom. "What do you think of these photos?"

Rows of families and couples and children were hanging from clothes pins along the perimeter of the walls. All taken at the bridge.

"You managed to snag a lot of customers."

"Good thing Ethan isn't my competition. I'm so jealous of his photographer's eye I could spit. But he does more nature stuff, not so much people."

"And he's pretty busy re-building a major historical landmark into a tourist attraction."

"Ah, so you've been out to the old Chaplin home. Actually, I think that house is his great-great-grandparents' home. They settled Heartland Cove in the early 1800s but I might be off by a decade or two."

"Doing your own personal research?" Allie said. Twinges of envy ate at her heart. What was wrong with her? She left Ethan with suspicions as wide as the Saint John River and now the thought of him and Marla deep in meaningful conversation made her want to pull out her hair because she wanted Ethan Smith to belong to her.

That was both sane and irrational, right?

Despite his words and mind-blowing kisses, Ethan didn't belong to her. But maybe she had that backwards. Ethan wanted to belong to her, but Allie's heart was still closed off, cracking open for a few brief moments when she contemplated life with a man like him.

Pushing him out of her thoughts as best she could, she spent the rest of the afternoon mounting the family photos for mailing with her old friend.

"I'll take care of ordering envelopes in mass quantity and bulk mailing so the cost doesn't absorb too much of the profits," Allie said. "And I'll start spreadsheets and do the tax paperwork. Oh, and we'll have to talk income and invoices and bookkeeping and how you want things filed."

"Good golly, Allie, all of that is such a headache! I'm so glad I don't have to worry about it."

"You only have to worry about being the artist. I'll be your manager and we'll live happily ever after."

"Done." They shook hands in mock fashion and then Marla glanced at the clock. "I get first dibs on the shower! We need to get out to Somerville for the wedding. Can you make sure I have my tripod packed downstairs in that pile by the front door?"

"Of course. Anything else?"

Marla kept talking as she headed through the hallway to the guest room bath. "I have a check list on the table. Good thing the rain from last night cleared up. If it was still threatening I'd be a wreck. My first wedding has to go perfectly. So much is riding on it for future customers."

"Go take your shower and be quick!"

Allie freshened her makeup and touched up her hair then grabbed her hand-bag and began loading the car with Marla's equipment. She decided to move the car closer to the house but couldn't find her keys anywhere, even dumping out her purse onto the bad to rummage through the usual purse clutter. It was nowhere to be found. Which also meant she had no house key, either. Had it fallen outside? There was no more time to search for it.

Nobody in tiny Heartland locked their doors, right? Despite tourists wandering around all summer.

Allie felt uneasy leaving the house open, but tried to reassure herself while she finished packing Marla's car. By the time they headed out of town, she'd put it out of her mind.

Marla was nervous, but it was a small wedding for a couple

that was remarrying for the second time, which calmed them both down. Still, there were pre-wedding photos, the ceremony in the backyard under an arbor, the wedding dinner, dancing, and some family groupings to snap.

It was almost eleven o'clock when they got home. Two small table lamps burned in the downstairs and upstairs hall, giving the appearance that someone was home. Everything appeared in perfect order—except for a gift basket left just inside the front door.

"Ethan," Allie said with a sigh.

"I'd love a gift basket from a man," Marla said. "Or an actual date. Or even a phone call."

"It's funny you say that because Ethan and I haven't actually dated."

"Yeah, you just lived with him."

"No, I didn't!" Allie protested. "I still have the rope and sheets to prove it, even if they're packed away in the linen closet now."

"Technicalities, my dear!" Marla said gaily. "And now I'm dragging my weary body to bed. Thank you for everything, sweetie. See you in the morning."

Allie grabbed a cold Diet Coke from the fridge and put the basket on the table to open, a small thrill going up her chest at the thought of a present.

But when she opened up the gift, it wasn't filled with gourmet cheeses or perfume or an engraved card inviting her to dinner, or anything romantic like that. It was filled with her mother's homemade bread and jam and vegetables from her parents' humongous summer garden. There was a lot of zucchini, of course.

A batch of Mom's extraordinary double chocolate brownies was the crowning glory.

"What the heck—" Allie shook her head, not getting it at all. She opened the card that wasn't completely sealed, the flap just tucked inside.

The basket was not for her at all. It was actually for Ethan. From her parents. They must assume he came by here regularly. Or they didn't know where he was staying now that he'd moved out. The note read:

"Dear Ethan,

This basket is a very small token of our eternal gratitude for purchasing the supplies we needed to rebuild the Strickland Family Fry business. You went above and beyond by delivering the materials as well as organizing the barn-raising, enlisting the entire town. We'll never forget this. The project has been daunting and overwhelming but we'll be back in business by the weekend and it's all because of your generosity.

We hope someday we can return the kindness, but an act we can never repay you for is when you rescued our daughter from the fire. You will always have a dear place in our lives and hearts.

Thank you.

Spencer and Phoebe Strickland

Allie's throat closed up with tears. *This* was the phone call Ethan had been trying to hide from her. A phone call from the lumber yard about her parents' fry shop. *He* had helped her parents. *He* had done this and hadn't wanted any thanks. He hadn't wanted Allie to feel obligated toward him.

Allie wept some more and reread the note. Oh, that Ethan Smith! What a dear, dear man.

Finally, she sniffed and rose from her chair. Even though she'd been on her feet all evening at the wedding—after running from a moose that afternoon—she paced the halls of the old house.

Remembering her lost keys, Allie tried once more to find them, but they were elusive and it was starting to drive her crazy.

Restless, Allie remembered that she had received a spare set of keys for the Victorian house from Viola Stark, but there was only one person who had them at the moment. Ethan Smith.

"I'm going out for a few minutes," Allie called through Marla's door. "Be back soon."

"Already asleep!" Marla called. "Be safe."

Allie revved the engine and tore out of the driveway with the gift basket on the seat next to her.

CHAPTER 22

Fairy lights—white Christmas lights—sparkled around the ramshackle Victorian that was known as the Heartbeat Inn.

Allie hurried up the steps of the wrap-around porch. Would she catch Ethan already in bed for the night? If so, she'd leave the basket at the front desk with a note. But boy, she really wanted to see him in person and give him an earful.

"Benjamin Ethan Miles," she said fiercely as she strode to the doors. "I'm about to give you a tongue lashing."

The B&B was lovely. She hadn't seen inside the place in ages. Not since the Christmas open house when she was about to graduate high school. The charming old hotel had been decorated to the nines, the scent of cinnamon wafting through the beautiful old halls.

After passing the blue reading room, Allie had to wait at the front desk until someone appeared. After all, it was after eleven o'clock now. Any sane person in Heartland would be home getting his or her rest so as to be ready to greet the first tourist bus in the morning.

"I need to deliver this basket to Ethan Smith," Allie told Mrs.

Simmons when she came around the corner. "And he has some keys I need."

The woman pursed her lips, lifting her eyes to the ceiling as if that would tell her whether or not Ethan was sound asleep or not.

"Room 204. Upstairs, second door on the left. Mind you, you can only stay a few minutes. And be *quiet.* I have a full house right now."

"Of course," Allie whispered. "Thanks." She tiptoed upstairs, smelling the chocolate wafting up from her mother's freshly baked brownies.

Despite knocking twice, nobody came to the door. While she waited, her eyes roved up and down the hallway, lit only with dim lights. She knocked one last time in case Ethan had been in the shower, but there was still no answer.

She hated to give up. She wanted her key, and she didn't want to leave her mother's gift in the hallway for someone to take.

Darting a glance around, Allie stealthily tried the door. She sucked in a breath when she realized that it was unlocked. Dare she push her way inside? The situation reminded her of when Ethan barged into her bathroom thinking the house was empty— and found a naked woman in the tub.

Allie's face burned with the memory, but lately she'd been having thoughts of sharing a Jacuzzi tub *with* Ethan.

Pushing at the door, Allie was inside two seconds later. At first, she feared she had the wrong room, but no, there was a suitcase of Ethan's things. She recognized his watch on the bedside table, a jacket lying on the bedspread, and a baseball cap she'd seen him wear while taking photos around town.

After flicking on the overhead light, she set the basket down on the table and let out a gasp. "Oh, oh, oh!" she cried softly, sinking to the edge of the bed.

All around the guests room, on every available space, lay rows and rows of pictures. Photographs, some framed, some mounted, some not. When she rose from the edge of the mattress, she touched the corners of the pictures with light fingers, her jaw dropping.

Every single photograph had been taken here in Heartland Cove: the bridge, the Victorian homes, the roads, the trees, the tourist area, gift shop, Fry Truck, lawns, river—and the people. Not just tourists, but photos of Heartland Cove residents. He'd captured them unaware, smiling, thoughtful, happy, sad. Every emotion portrayed poignantly in startling clarity. The pictures were emotional and heartfelt and a work of art.

As Allie studied them it became apparent that one particular thread ran through them all—the powerful love Ethan had for the town and people of Heartland Cove, and it rendered her speechless.

Her throat closed up and Allie wanted to weep at their beauty.

A sudden creak at the door made her whirl around.

Ethan stood at the door, going still at the sight of her in his room, shock all over his face. Allie's body stiffened, afraid he'd be angry to catch her looking at his photographs, but it was too late to hide.

"Ethan," Allie whispered. "Why didn't you tell me?"

He frowned with uncertainty. "What are you doing here? Are you upset? Do you still think I'm in cahoots with Mayor Jefferies? Allie, please believe me that I'm not—"

Allie rushed at him, throwing her arms around his neck. "I believe you," she said with a laugh that instantly turned into tears again.

"Are you all right?" he asked. "Why are you crying? What's happened?"

"Oh, Ethan, these aren't the pictures of someone who wants to ruin Heartland Cove. These are the pictures of someone who wants to preserve every corner, every person, and every tidbit of history. It all makes sense why you and Miss Ellie are building the historical center. You truly do love this place, don't you?"

"It sounds sappy, but I do." His eyes caught sight of the basket on the table, sitting in the midst of a group of photos of his grandmother at her home in the garden, white hair sparkling, laughing up at the sky with crinkled eyes. "What's this?" he asked.

"A gift from my parents."

"You came all the way to the B&B to give me a basket from your mother?"

Allie's face burned and she adding sheepishly, "And I need a key for the house. I lost mine."

"Here, take this one. I'll get a new copy made at the hardware store." He lifted the card from its position on the loaf of homemade bread and read it. His eyes fastened to hers and he pressed his lips together. "Did you read this?"

"I'm sorry. My parents left it at the house, not knowing where you were staying. It was there when I got home from the wedding with Marla. I read it before I knew what it was."

"I see," he said cautiously.

"Oh, Ethan, you wonderful, incredible man," Allie said quietly. "*You* rebuilt my parents' business. That was the phone call today at the construction site. I was afraid you were still keeping secrets from me."

"I could see that in your face, and it worried me. I will never keep secrets from you. But I don't usually broadcast all my deeds." He let out a small laugh.

"You mean your generous, good, and thoughtful deeds?"

"It's not that much—" he began.

"Ethan Smith, it means everything to my parents—and to me."

Allie stepped forward and Ethan's arms encircled her as she wrapped her arms around his waist, pressing her face into his shoulder. *"Thank you. For everything."*

He held her tight, without speaking, for several long moments. The world felt so right inside his arms, so perfect. She never wanted to be away from him again.

Ethan cupped his palms around her face, staring deep into her eyes. "Allie Strickland, I know it's probably too fast and too soon, but I love you. I want to be with you forever, but I'll be patient. Even if it takes years, you're worth the wait."

"You're not worried that I'll only want you for your money?"

He lifted her up in his arms to whirl her about the room. "Not worried at all. You kissed me when you thought I was a lowly, scheming photographer. And now you're always taunting me about being rich, as if money is evil, when I'm still, at the moment, very much poor."

"Money isn't evil exactly," Allie said, wrinkling her nose. "It's just that Sean was always talking about money and how rich we were going to be and I just did not care."

"Well, I also might have a secret conniving brother who steals it away from me. Just like out of that *Sense and Sensibility* movie."

"You know about Jane Austen?"

"Of course. If you're going to be my girl—my wife—I'd better know all the things you love and can't live without. Like Godiva chocolate imported from New York City when the entire stock of Laura Secord is sold out."

Leaning in, Allie pressed her lips against his soft, warm, and perfect mouth, savoring the way he made her feel. She was about to explode with a thousand emotions she couldn't even begin to name. "I'm not sure I can live without you any longer either, Mr. Ethan Smith," she murmured against his lips. "Or should I call you Benji?"

He pulled back to give her a smirk. "You can forget the Benji part—but the rest of what you just said . . . that's what I call the best thing I've heard all day."

And then he kissed her, deeply and ardently, and Allie was sure she never wanted to stop.

CHAPTER 23

A few days later, Allie unpacked the box that held her wedding dress. The left-over invitations, the engraved napkins, and the favors tied with lace.

She called Marla to the backyard and together they fed every single item into a fifty-gallon drum crackling with bright orange flames. Allie watched her old wedding paraphernalia go up in smoke and ashes. From this day forward Sean Carter didn't exist.

Except for the diamond engagement ring she'd taken off the day she arrived in Heartland Cove after leaving Toronto. That little item she hocked in the next town over. And the pawn shop owner said it wasn't worth half what Sean had told her it was worth.

Despite the catch in her throat, Allie was not surprised.

TWO WEEKS LATER, *Marla's Magical Moments* officially celebrated its grand opening with an open house and an advertisement in the local papers.

Almost two hundred people came to celebrate and eat cake

and peruse the old Victorian house decorated with Marla's photographs. Marla christened the beautiful hanging sign by breaking a bottle of champagne across it, and the crowd cheered.

At the end of the party, when the house was filled with empty paper plates and the trash bin was overflowing, Ethan made an announcement. "I have a final gift for your grand opening, ladies."

"You didn't have to get us a gift," Allie said, clapping her hands. "But what is it?"

Marla was half-asleep on the couch. "You open it, Allie. I don't plan on moving for at least twenty-four hours."

Ethan handed over a white envelope. "I'm actually giving you something I can't use any longer. And it's really old. And needs some repairs."

"A card?" Allie cocked one eyebrow. "You're talking in riddles."

"Everything you need to know is in the card," Ethan said, feigning a yawn to make it look like nothing.

Immediately suspicious, Allie slit open the envelope, and pulled out a cream-colored card engraved with gold calligraphy.

Out loud she read, "I hereby gift the house in which you presently stand to Allie Strickland and Marla Perry for their own, to have and to hold forever, for as long as *Marla's Magical Moments* survives."

"Very funny, Ethan. You can't give us an entire house. We'd planned on paying rent beginning in September."

"It's mine to give and you need a place of business, you two. I predict much success. And Marla can move into the upstairs master suite."

"You adorable man!" Allie said. She stared down at the card giving them the unimaginable gift of an entire house. "Are you serious?"

"Deadly," Ethan answered, trying not to grin.

THE NEIGHBOR'S SECRET

Marla hugged him. "You're—you're—amazing, but I can't accept an entire house from you."

"Well, it's not a house, it's a business, and I'm certainly not going to live here."

"Okaaaay." Tears sprang to Marla's eyes. "But I think you're nuts to give away an entire house."

"Easier than trying to cut it in half," Ethan dead-panned.

Marla threw a pillow at him from across the room, then snatched up the gift card and pressed it to her chest.

"But where will I live?" Allie asked, biting at her lips to keep from grinning, too.

"With me in my house—the house we're going to buy—or build—when we get married."

Allie fluttered her eyelashes at him, one hand on her hips. "And when will that be, pray tell?"

"As soon as you say yes and pick a date. Preferably by Christmas because I can't wait."

Allie leaned in and kissed him. "You're just like a little kid. Are we getting sleds for Christmas, too?"

"Now that you mention it, yes. But pretend to be surprised when you see them under the tree."

After another round of celebrating, Marla rose from the couch and dragged herself to bed. The house quieted as streetlights flickered on one by one.

Ethan took Allie by the arm, circling her waist with his hand. "Let's go for a walk. There's something I've been wanting to do for a very long time."

Arm in arm, they walked out the door of the house and along the evening streets of Heartland Cove. The town was still, holding its breath like a cat about to pounce a mouse under the sliver of new moon.

New moons, new beginnings, Allie mused, her fingers entwined with Ethan's.

They passed dark houses, listening to the sound of a dog snuffling in someone's yard, the hoot of an owl overhead. Up ahead, the river was a black ribbon, the lights of the bridge beckoning them forward.

"As long as it isn't a moose," Allie whispered, and Ethan stifled a snort of laughter.

It was about a mile to the Heartland Bridge—and despite the exterior lights to warn motorists, the interior was dark as Hades at midnight.

Snuggling into Ethan's shoulder, Allie laughed, feeling like she was a kid again, out late at night to meet friends for Kick the Can, or to stretch along the grass of the riverfront when they were teenagers and bored to death while naming the constellations.

"Here," Ethan said when they reached the pavement of the road that led inside.

Allie followed Ethan inside the bridge as he tugged her along. "Where are we going?" she asked.

"You'll see soon enough."

The only sound was the shushing noise of the river running underneath the pilings as they moved forward with slow, cautious steps.

"I can't even see it's so dark in here," Allie whispered. "What if a car comes?"

"Nobody crosses the river at midnight. Don't you know it's the time for lovers?"

"Is that what we are?" Allie said, leaning in to kiss the warm spot under his chin.

"Not yet, my girl," he said. "But hurry!"

They kept walking, hanging on to each other, and then Ethan said, "This is it. Right here. We are now standing directly in the center of the bridge."

His voice echoed in the cavernous bridge, sounding just like they were in a tunnel.

"How do you know for sure we're in the middle?"

THE NEIGHBOR'S SECRET

Allie could have sworn that Ethan blushed at the question, despite the darkness.

"I came earlier to scout it out and mark how many steps it was," he admitted, tightening his grip on her hand as they walked.

"You adorable man," Allie said, touched at the attention to detail he'd taken to making tonight perfect.

The smell of the water and grassy rushes rose up around them, the gurgling of the Saint John's running below them in the darkness.

A dark blue sky dotted with brilliant stars illuminated the sky through the cavernous opening of the bridge.

"I can hear the waterfall moving below us," Allie said. "Fish jumping. It sounds magical." She glanced behind her in the opposite direction—to that world far beyond their small town. "Are you *sure* we're not going to get run over by a sudden, speeding truck filled with reckless teenagers?"

Ethan laughed. "Positive. Because tonight my dream is coming true. I get to kiss Allie Strickland in the middle of the Heartland Cove bridge at midnight. I've been waiting a long time for this, you know. More than ten years."

"You're a mighty patient man, Ethan Smith."

"I think my patience is about to be rewarded," he murmured, taking her in his arms and pressing his lips against hers.

Allie clasped her arms around his neck, her heart racing, her temperature rising. Ethan pulled her closer, his hand on the back of her head as they kissed and kissed and kissed in the evening of a long summer's day.

Absolutely nothing in the world was better than kissing Ethan Smith at midnight on the Heartland Cove County Bridge.

∽

A week after returning from their honeymoon to Prince Edward Island, Allie and Ethan sat amidst the torn-up walls and the new foundation of the Heartland County Historical Society's site.

Piles of fresh lumber gave off a sharp, pungent tang in the crisp afternoon. Snow drifts still piled under the woody pines, but an unexpected day of sunshine had melted the area around the house and the new roof kept the two newlyweds from completely freezing.

Bundled in her coat, mittens, and hat, Allie gave a wave when she spotted a car sputtering up the drive.

A minute later, Marla stepped out, slamming the door and carrying a large gift bag in her hand. "You two are insane! You're going to lose your toes out here it's so cold! You do realize that it's January, right?"

Allie jumped up to give her friend a hug. The signature scent of Marla was now film developing fluid and fresh-cut paper. "What are you doing all the way out here?"

"I just got the pictures developed from your wedding and couldn't wait to show you. Plus, I have great news. I'm in cahoots with Ava at Heartland Inn. She offers wedding package stays at the B&B, but we're now teaming up to include *Marla's Magical Moments* as part of the package to couples. Hopefully that will help both of our businesses."

"That's fantastic, Marla!" Allie said, reaching out to embrace her. "I guess we're both staying in Heartland Cove for a while, eh?"

Marla gave an amused snort. "Never saw it coming, but now all I need to do is import a devastatingly handsome billionaire and life will be perfect."

"Stranger things have happened," Allie said, stifling secret amusement.

Marla reached into her bag with a rustle of paper and tissue. "Okay, so I know I gave you a set of crockery as a gift—practical and boring. But this is my real wedding gift to you. And my favorite, of course."

She pulled out a thick plush album chock full of vibrant

pictures of Heartland Cove on the day of their wedding. People smiling and laughing and eating and toasting Allie and Ethan.

Joy burst out of the pictures and Allie laughed, even as tears filled her eyes at the memories and emotion displayed in the photos. "I'm blown away. These are absolutely perfect."

"Here's the best photo," Marla said. "I had it framed in Montreal. The guy at the shop did a gorgeous job."

Indeed, it was. The beveled matting was a gold color and the frame was gilded in an antique finish.

The photo was an image of Ethan and Allie gazing out at the bridge, hand in hand. Allie's white wedding dress billowed about her, veil flying in an unseen breeze, while Ethan looked devastatingly gorgeous in a black tux and tails. It was a perfect shot against a bright blue sky that defied weather logic on Christmas Eve, despite the fresh snow in drifts about their feet.

Allie remembered how cold she'd been that day and by the time they returned to the reception she couldn't feel her toes. Taking pictures was a frantic venture, and most of them had been done indoors, but both of them wanted a photo in their wedding finery at the Heartland Cove County Bridge.

"I love it so much, Marla," Allie told her. "Thank you, it's perfect."

She sighed, glancing up at Ethan with glistening eyes as he pressed his lips to her forehead. "A dream come true, my beautiful wife," he said softly.

In the photograph, she and Ethan's hands were clasped tightly together, eyes focused on the distant shore. As if their future had suddenly opened up in a vision only the two of them could see. A future bright and clear, and filled with the deepest, most unexpected love.

∽

EPILOGUE

LOCAL ELECTIONS

Mayor Jefferies made a statement to the press today that he will not be running for reelection next year.

ADVERTISEMENT

*I*n celebration of Allie Strickland and Ethan Smith AKA Benjamin Ethan Miles', marriage, the Strickland Family Fry Shop is having a *Half off Special* on shrimp and burgers—and the tastiest seasoned fries in New Brunswick!

∼

HE WAS A JUVENILE DELINQUENT. **She was an aspiring pianist. When sparks fly at their high school reunion, they're willing to forget the past—until old secrets surface, threatening to destroy their future.**

Does Caleb have a chance to win Kira's heart—or will his fami-

ly's hidden secret prevent him from capturing the girl who got away?

READ the next title in the *Secret Billionaire Romance Series* right now: One click takes you to:

THE EXECUTIVE'S SECRET!

AUTHOR'S NOTE

Dear Romance Lover,

I hope you enjoyed reading *The Neighbor's Secret: A Secret Billionaire Romance!* Please check out my other sweet romance novels on Amazon, too. They're all FREE on Kindle Unlimited as well.

If you'd like to be the first to hear about new releases, giveaways, or extras, subscribe to my Reader's Club Newsletter and never miss a thing! Subscribe now and you will receive two FREE books!

Warmest wishes,

~Kimberley Montpetit

∽

I also write the award-winning FORBIDDEN trilogy (HarperCollins) and Scholastic Middle-Grade novels under the name:

~Kimberley Griffiths Little

AUTHOR'S NOTE

Find all these titles on Amazon, Barnes & Noble, your local bookstore, and on my website:
   www.KimberleyGriffithsLittle.com

ABOUT THE AUTHOR

Kimberley Montpetit once spent all her souvenir money at the *La Patisserie* shops when she was in Paris—on the arm of her adorable husband. The author grew up in San Francisco, but currently lives in a small town along the Rio Grande with her big, messy family.

Kimberley reads a book a day and loves to travel. She's stayed in the haunted tower room at Borthwick Castle in Scotland, sailed the Seine in Paris, ridden a camel among the glorious cliffs of Petra, shopped the maze of the Grand Bazaar in Istanbul, and spent the night in an old Communist hotel in Bulgaria.

Find all of Kimberley's Novels Here on Amazon

Get FREE Books when you subscribe to Kimberley's Newsletter

www.KimberleyMonpetit.com

ALSO BY KIMBERLEY MONTPETIT

Catch the bestselling series set in Snow Valley, Montana

Risking it all for Love

Romancing Rebecca

Sealed with a Kiss

UnBreak my Heart

The Secret of a Kiss

All 5 books in a boxed set!

Love in Snow Valley, The Complete Collection

Read the bestselling *Secret Billionaire Romance* series!

The Neighbor's Secret

The Executive's Secret

The Mafia's Secret

The Owner's Secret

The Billionaire's Christmas Hideaway

The Fiance's Secret

Purchase all of Kimberley's Romance Novels HERE

Go Here to get a FREE book as a gift from Kimberley!

SNEAK PEEK THE EXECUTIVE'S SECRET BY KIMBERLEY MONTPETIT

CHAPTER 1

Caleb Davenport gripped his briefcase, sliding out of the hired car paid for by the company account. After a transatlantic flight it was a relief not having to worry about throwing a few twenty dollar bills at the driver, or digging out his credit card. He strode toward the double glass doors of the high-rise club in downtown Denver.

Breathing in the crisp fall air, Caleb finally relaxed, even though he was jet-lagged after making the transfer from Hong Kong via Los Angeles.

He was home, and the Rocky Mountains exuded their own sweet, familiar scent. The high altitude was bracing, clean and fresh. No more stifling hot, crowded streets with a hundred different scents of food vendors, perfumes, and body odor.

Eager to meet up with the rest of the partners of DREAMS, Caleb punched the elevator button for the ninth floor. His stomach grumbled demanding food. Maybe he and the rest of the guys should have met up over dinner. It was later than he'd thought and the small sandwich on the plane hours ago hadn't exactly been filling.

Waiting for his luggage had taken longer than expected, too, and on this particular Friday night Denver's downtown streets were packed with taxis, rental cars, the 16th Street mall shuttle, as well as the Light Rail commuter train coming in and out of the convention center tracks. A couple of busses rumbled past, filled with name tag wearing folks. Must be some big conventions going on this weekend.

Personally, Caleb was convention-ed out. Three of them back-to-back overseas with more than a dozen companies signing onto the hot new app. His baby, DREAMS; the computer site and app he'd spent years working on.

All in all, the past week had been a resounding success. His little company had grown by leaps and bounds over the past few years, serving thousands of consumers with insanely inexpensive products around the world.

It was mind-blowing to think he was going to bank close to a billion dollars by the end of the year—and it all started with his group of high school computer geek friends.

Caleb's pace turned brisk when he pushed through the glass doors into the posh vestibule of the bar. The five of them; Troy, Brandon, Ryan, Adam, and himself, sent each other a deluge of text messages while overseas—but they often didn't convey many details. Even more often were missing text messages. As if they disappeared traveling through long distance phone lines in third world countries.

The one message that had managed to get through to everyone was his invitation to celebrate at their favorite bar.

"**Meet me at *The 54*,**" he'd texted and, like a ten-thousand-mile miracle from across the Pacific Ocean, he'd received four thumbs up from his partners.

At the end of the plush carpeted vestibule, Caleb opened the second glass door that spelled out *The 54* in swirly gold letters. He was greeted by the hostess, a woman of about twenty-five dressed in a black dress that shimmered from a luminescent fabric. Sleeveless, plunging neckline, the woman had a terrific figure, and toned arms as if she had an exercise trainer.

"Good evening, sir. Welcome to *The 54*," she purred in a cultured voice with a slight accent. Italian? English? He couldn't quite detect her country of origin, although he should, he'd been to London and Rome often enough the past few years on business. "Do you have a reservation with us tonight?"

"Reservation's under Caleb Davenport."

The hostess placed a red manicured finger on her wait list. A small lamp on the tall desk illuminating the ledger with a golden glow.

"I have you right here, Mr. Davenport," she said. "Please follow me."

When she sashayed Caleb to his reserved table in the back, he noted the shapely legs in five-inch high stilettos. With the heels, she was still much shorter than Caleb, who, at six feet four often came across as a big, lumbering bear, even while keeping in shape by running five miles every day. She couldn't be more than five feet two. Despite the attractive women he ran into making business deals and traveling, most women were too short for his taste. He'd love a girl who was closer to five foot ten or taller, actually. Someone he could dance cheek-to-cheek with. A woman he could kiss without breaking his back.

Of course, Caleb wasn't planning to hit on *The 54's* hostess, despite her beauty and lovely accent. But once again, whenever he saw a woman he admired, Caleb instantly found himself thinking about the woman he did want. The woman he wanted for his wife and the mother of his children. Someone to share all this—this crazy life—the money—the travel. And yes, the burden.

Having DREAMS thrive so quickly was often disorienting. When he returned home, Caleb had to purposely ground himself by spending time with his best friends. He'd eat at his favorite restaurants, kick-back at home with a Jason Bourne flick, sit outdoors at the Red Rocks Amphitheater for a concert, or take a hike in the pine forests.

And, of course, make a visit to his parents. Despite the pain that visit brought. Tonight he was feeling guilty, knowing he hadn't visited them in nearly a year. It was too difficult, emotionally distracting, and exhausting, but his mother's birthday was coming up and she'd never forgive him if he didn't bring himself bearing a gift.

It might be crazy to make a list of what he wanted in a woman, but when the hostess showed him their table for five and laid out their menus, Caleb realized he could practically reach down and pat her on the head like she was twelve-years-old. Girls who could wear heels and look him in the eye were hard to find, but a definite priority for his "list". Harder to find in the Asian countries he was currently visiting setting up accounts for DREAMS. Idly, Caleb wondered if women were taller in London where Troy usually traveled. He'd have to ask, he thought, and then grinned to himself.

Pushing thirty, Caleb was ready to find *the* woman. A woman he could spend the rest of his life with. His business and travel didn't leave much time for dating. Let alone women he could talk to without an interpreter. Even if they spoke English and he loved their accent, it wasn't the same. Whether it was books or music or movies or favorite foods, they had little in common.

Caleb gave a sigh and dropped his briefcase to the floor by the table, glancing about for any sign of his team.

The 54 was quieter than most upscale Denver club for the rich citizens of this city. And for him, having a membership here was a reality that was hard to calibrate with his old life.

When Caleb stared at the art deco on the walls, the polished 1920s furnishings, and the painted ceilings, he felt like an outsider.

Heck, he'd grown up in a poor neighborhood, attended a passable elementary school, but fortunate that it fed into a better high school. His father had been a drunken mechanic working odd jobs at home, his mother a part-time school aide who kept her husband company at night with the bottle.

At ten years old, he used to dream of buying them a new house one day. A house that wasn't hanging together with duct tape. Mostly because *he* was the one who wanted to escape his depressing life. He never had friends over. Never told anyone where he lived.

Sitting here now in a posh bar was so diametrically opposite to how he'd grown up that his life felt surreal. As if he could blink his eyes and it would all disappear like a dream.

"Hey, buddy, what are you doing here?" a voice came from behind, echoing his thoughts uncannily.

He whipped around to see Troy Thurlow, his best friend since high school, barreling toward him. "Hey yourself."

"They let riffraff in these places now?" Troy teased.

"Nope, I sneaked in. Like usual."

"That's what I figured," Troy plopped into a seat and grabbed the drink menu.

Caleb still had moments where Troy's friendship and their partnership in DREAMS felt bizarre. But the two of them discovered they had a talent for calculus and computers so they'd end up at the Thurlow home doing math homework while watching *Breaking Bad*, and surreptitiously studied the cheerleaders during lunch in the quad.

Caleb was the greasy geek of the school. A loner who purposely stayed under the radar in the computer lab, except for moments with Troy—when he was virtually invisible next to the vastly more popular football player. There were times during high school that Caleb had wondered if he was Troy's pity project, or a dare. Now he didn't know what he was. Still a geek? Finally grown up when he turned twenty-nine in January?

"Looks like you're overthinking things as usual," Troy said, slapping him on the shoulder.

Caleb gave a snort. "What makes you say that?"

"Your expression was very studious. Bad flight home?"

"Nope, completely uneventful. Just . . . thinking, like you always say."

"It's a woman, isn't it?" Troy gave a grin, waggling his eyebrows. "Who'd you meet in Hong Kong?"

"Nobody," Caleb burst out with a laugh.

"The airline attendant must have been hot then."

Without warning, Brandon appeared and slid into a chair. "You met a babe flight attendant? Tell us more."

Caleb let out a longer laugh. "I couldn't even tell you what the flight attendants looked like. Short? Dark hair? Polite? Served food and drinks. End of story."

Brandon flipped open a menu. "Here I was all ready for a juicy story."

"You mean you didn't meet the woman of your dreams in Brazil, Brandon?" Troy kicked back in his seat and placed his hands behind his head after signaling to the waitress.

"Next time please send me to Rio during Mardi Gras," Brandon told Caleb.

"Nothin' doin'. You'd never come home again."

"There are perks to this job, right?" Troy went on. "But, no, our boss is all work, work, work. I spend the other half of my life sitting on planes."

"Welcome to the real world," Ryan Argyle said, coming up to the table and bumping fists with the rest of the men. Right on his heels was the last member of the DREAMS team, Adam Caldwell, pulling off his tie and unbuttoning the top button of a crisp blue shirt.

"Good, we're finally all here," Caleb said. "Now we can order."

"Hey, I came as soon as I shut down the office," Adam said. "I work longer hours than all of you put together, flying around the world, dancing with luscious foreign women at night."

"Hardly," Troy said with a glance upward at the waitress, a

thin woman of about thirty-five wearing black slacks, a black blouse and thick black eyeliner. "I'll have a ginger ale."

The other guys laughed and Caleb held up his hands to ward off their teasing. "A Coke with vanilla," he said. "And keep the nachos coming, please. Mini sliders, too."

"What's with all the fizzy drinks, guys?" Ryan said. "I know Caleb doesn't touch anything hard, but what about the rest of you guys?"

"Headache," Troy said. "Jet lag is getting to me. I can't even remember what time zone I'm in."

"Mountain Time, poor baby," Adam interjected. "Try sitting at a desk logging orders and shipments until your eyes go numb. I'll have a cold beer, please."

"Didn't know eyes could turn numb," Caleb laughed, giving the youngest member of their crew a teasing grin. Adam Caldwell had been in the class a year behind them in high school. But his computer skills were ferocious so Caleb had hired him two years ago. "That's a new one."

He'd known these guys for so long, but what most of them forgot—except for Troy—was the fact that Caleb never drank. He'd grown up with alcoholic parents and after binge-drinking at a party his senior year, he'd passed out and wouldn't wake up. Terrified, Troy had called an ambulance, afraid Caleb was going to die from alcohol poisoning.

Caleb would never forget his mother speaking at his hospital bedside in a soft voice. "Isn't it bad enough that your father does this?"

She'd been so hurt, her tired face so full of despair, that Caleb hadn't touched a drink since. Despite the teasing during college, the parties going on at his dorm, he just *didn't*. It wasn't worth it. Besides, he wanted to live rather than get a buzz. And avoid liver damage like his father was now suffering with.

Troy ran his hands through his thick dark hair, slouching back in his chair. He was a big man, wide shouldered, with a chest as broad as a football field. Played wide receiver during high school at their alma mater, Southfield High School, but loved the intricacies of computer hardware. He was the guy that could trouble-shoot anything. "Man, it's good to be home."

"Homesick, buddy?" Adam teased.

Troy gave a half smile, shrugging. "There's something about the fall mountain air of Denver that clears your head. South America is just hot and sticky, no matter what time of year you visit."

"Speaking of autumn, what month are we in?" Ryan said, scrolling a thumb across his phone screen. "I've been in too many time zones to remember."

"Months—times zones—it's all the same, oh brainy one," Caleb said, and then added, "Just turned October. We have to hit the office tomorrow, guys. It's only Tuesday and we've got a boatload of data to enter and organize and get on the app."

"Yeah, yeah, we know boss," Troy said, stuffing a burger slider into his mouth now. "You don't have to remind us."

September had proven to be a grueling month and the guys were just doing their usual complaining when they put in an eighty-hour work week during travel but some days he hated being the CEO. They'd known each since their teens, and it often was uncomfortable to be their boss, having to crack the whip with his high school friends.

Ryan dipped a tortilla chip into the nacho cheese dip. "Only asking because I just remembered that we have our ten-year high school reunion later this month."

"We couldn't possibly be that old," Troy quipped, picking up his second slider in under sixty seconds. "Wasn't it only last June that we graduated?"

Ryan gave Troy an eye roll. "Oh, wise one, thank you for that. Did your invitations arrive in the mail? I think it's being held at the Hotel Monaco on Champa Street. Dinner and a DJ, of course. No host bar."

"Ooh, fancy," Adam said. "They must think we're rich."

Low chuckles erupted around the table while Troy said, "Hopefully they don't make us play any stupid games. I'll never forget our senior picnic. Getting dragged in the mud during the tug of war."

"You should have hung on," Caleb teased him.

"If I recall the food was good," Brandon added. "Never-ending barbecue and pie."

"To you, the food is always good," Troy told him. "You have a bottomless pit for a stomach. Your travel reimbursement for restaurants is astronomical."

"Have we made a pact to go—or not?" Ryan asked. "Don't want to show up alone and make small talk with people I don't recognize."

Caleb had forgotten about the reunion, actually. It wasn't in his planner. He shook the hair out of his eyes and stared around the table. All the guys were gazing at him. Like he was the boss of the high school reunion, too. "We could draw straws," he said with a half smile.

"Better than tossing a coin," Adam said, pulling out his calculator to figure out the odds.

An odd shiver ran through Caleb. Recalling the insane stuff that had happened with his parents during high school still felt surreal. He'd basically been on his own since seventeen, but instead of a fierce independence without having to care about anybody but himself, the opposite had happened.

Traveling the world, making bigger bucks than he could ever have dreamed, had produced a lonely, untethered life. Sure, he could do whatever he wanted, but running a company on which hundreds of employees relied on you in twenty different countries, including a team of accountants and lawyers watching your every move created stress that was also far greater than he could have imagined.

He relied on the men sitting around the dinner table very

much. Not just for business, but for friendship and support, saving him from total loneliness. They'd certainly become his surrogate family, and having the support of his friends meant that he avoided obsessing about the past and his derelict parents—except for one person that had never left his memory.

The girl he'd had a crush on since he was a freshman. English class. Staring at the back of her head like a dunce. Caleb sat two desks behind her, fantasizing about running his hands through the silky strands of her shiny hair that swayed along her shoulders and down her back like a waterfall. Yeah, typical teenage boy stuff.

But that girl was untouchable. Far above his low class life. She was soft-spoken and gentle with a laugh that used to make him smile. She wasn't annoying or loud like most girls in high school, vying for attention or queen bee status. She was perfect. The kind of girl you could fall in love with and live happily ever after—if there was such a thing. Unfortunately, he didn't know many happily ever after's. None of his friends were married. A few of his international clients were happily divorced or living up the bachelor life.

He must be the most peculiar man out there to crave a traditional marriage and family. A house that smelled of fresh baked cookies and filled with people who loved each other and didn't have yelling matches or drunken stupors.

There were a lot of reasons Caleb used to hide out in the computer lab, learning C++. When he created computer games it was like submerging himself under water. He could be immune from the world until the janitor kicked him out.

But *that girl* topped the list of reasons. Seeing her every day made him drown with a desire like a vice squeezing at his heart. Caleb just made sure he didn't drool on his desk.

The most bizarre thing was the fact that he still thought about her. More than ten years later. Images would flash through his mind of her standing at her locker spinning the combination lock. In the cafeteria thoughtfully eating fries. Bent over a class assignment, scribbling furiously while her satin hair draped her arm.

He'd get up to sharpen a pencil just so he could sneak a peek at her touching the tip of her tongue on her top lip in concentration, erasing a line, rummaging in her purse, or drumming her slender fingers on the desk as if practicing piano scales. Everything about her mesmerized him.

So, the question was, would *she* be at the class reunion?

Caleb gulped down his drink, inwardly shaking his head at his idiocy.

She was probably married and had three kids. Plus, a mortgage and an accountant for a husband in the ritzy suburb of Greenwood Village.

Of course, maybe she'd moved far away, like California, South Dakota, or Florida.

For all he knew, she could be serving as a Red Cross nurse in Africa.

When Caleb discovered the high school reunion notice in his mail a couple of months ago, fresh hope had lodged firmly in his throat.

"Hey, earth to Caleb, earth to Caleb," Troy said punching him on the arm.

Startled, Caleb knocked over his glass, soda drizzling across the white tablecloth. He grabbed napkins and blotted it out. "Hey, watch it," he joked in an attempt to hide his daydreaming.

"You alright, Mr. Boss?" Ryan said, motioning to the waitress for more napkins and a fresh drink for Caleb.

"I'm fine," Caleb said, glancing around the table at his co-workers. "Never better."

"Jet lag, I tell you," Brandon said. "Especially when you've been in Hong Kong. It's the worst. You lose a day, you gain a day. Over and over again."

Deftly, their waitress served a fresh glass of soda and ice, mopped up the spill, and then scooped up handfuls of soggy napkins.

Adam stared after her retreating figure, obviously wishing he could flirt with her. The guy flirted with every female within ten feet.

"So," Caleb said, glancing around the table. Most of the food was gone, but he dipped a tortilla chip into the last of the salsa with a nonchalant air. "Everybody going to the reunion, then?"

Adam snorted and Ryan cocked an eyebrow. "Yeah, Mr. Boss. Five minutes ago, we decided we were all going together. Stag. It'll give us a chance to check out the girls who broke our hearts ten years ago. Fourteen years for old Troy here since he's been dopey about some girl since his freshman year. Now I call that pathetic."

Caleb gave a forced laugh, hoping the guys hadn't noticed that he'd missed the last thread of the conversation. He reached for the menu, still hungry. "Where's our waitress?"

"You just zoned out," Troy said, staring at him. "We're leaving *The 54* and just waiting for the check. We decided we need real food so we're going to *Rossi's* for dinner. This was just appetizers."

"Okay." Caleb wondered if he could stay awake. "Haven't been to *Rossi's* in ages."

The check came and he stuck his American Express on the plastic plate. The waitress whisked it away and was back again in moments. Caleb scribbled his signature and rose, suddenly needing fresh air.

The other guys filed out noisily, talking, catching up, while Caleb followed, tucking his wallet into his back pocket.

It was only eight o'clock. He'd look like a wimp if he went home without treating the guys to a nice dinner after their ten days of travel. It was a tradition, actually. But man, he was dead tired. What was wrong with him?

A stupid question. It was the class reunion. The thought of it depressed him. He could imagine getting dressed up, making the effort, only to find out *she* was living in a village in Bulgaria teaching English to eight-year-olds.

The October air was brisk, smacking him in the face while they congregated around the taxi circle in front of *The 54*. The bar's sign blared a bright neon blue behind them while they waited for a taxi to come around the block.

Standing just outside the circle of light spilling from the lobby, Caleb surreptitiously reached into his wallet and flipped open the billfold. Tonight's talk had made him nostalgic.

Inside the leather billfold was a small compartment. For years, he'd kept a secret within the small pouch—a dainty chain of silver with a red ruby dangling from the bottom.

He'd kept the necklace with him for almost eleven years. Ever since she'd accidentally dropped it the middle of their senior year and he'd snatched it up.

Caleb didn't take it out very often. The necklace was one part guilty pleasure, the other part pure guilt that he'd never returned it.

While clenching the necklace in his fist, a taxi pulled up and the other four guys piled in, leaving the shot-gun spot free for their CEO.

"Let's hit the road," he heard them call while the vehicle's doors slammed shut and the engine idled, waiting for him.

Caleb slipped the ruby necklace with its two small diamonds back into the tiny pouch of the billfold, jammed it into his rear pocket, and clenched the handle of his briefcase.

Enough was enough. He had to return it. It was wrong to have kept it. But first he had to find the girl who used to wear it, the red gemstone dangling in the air when she hovered over her math homework in the corner of Algebra class. Far away from him.

Over the years, he'd run into old classmates at the movies, or at restaurants. But never her.

Not that he hadn't made an attempt. He'd looked all right. Her parents were still in the phone book but on a different street than where she had grown up.

But she wasn't listed.

And she wasn't on Facebook.

He was too embarrassed to reach out to her old friends. Or to call her parents.

Even though they'd been in classes together, off and on, she had never given him a second glance. Heck, he would have died and gone to heaven for a first glance, but he'd been a geek in every sense of the word. Frizzy hair. Dorky glasses. Nerdy jeans that never fit properly, bought at second-hand shops, and perpetually hiding his family's secrets from the world.

Years had become a decade.

Caleb gave a snort of self derision. Wow, his lack of confidence when it came to women had become a numbing force that froze him into limbo.

"Where to?" the cab driver asked, pulling into traffic.

"*Rossi's*," Caleb said, noticing how the other guys let him answer. Deferring to him as the boss. It was still odd, even after five years.

Her necklace had become a memento of his stupid high school years, but she was lost to time and distance.

How did you get over a girl you never had in the first place?

A small surge of hope rose up his throat. Would she be at the high school reunion? It might be his only—and last—chance.

Grab the rest of THE EXECUTIVE'S SECRET HERE, Free on Kindle Unlimited.

Made in United States
Cleveland, OH
29 October 2024